Truth or Daire

Love and Embezzlement Book One

Marty Vee

Newsletter Fun!

♥

I love my newsletter, it's my favorite way to connect with my readers. Stay in the know about exciting news, upcoming releases, fun stuff, and freebies.

https://www.subscribepage.com/martyvee

Contents

Dedication

♥

Andrew V.
You're my favorite person and the love of my life, and I'm obsessed with you... In a not creepy way.

Chapter One

♥

Serena

My flowy robin's egg blue skirt was the wrong choice. After months of heavy winter clothing, I wanted to wear something that felt like the spring tulips blooming along the Magnificent Mile. Something that felt like shedding the grayscale of the long winter, and the layers that were now firmly left behind in last season.

I should have stuck with my normal tasteful slacks and blazer. The wind gusting off of Lake Michigan threatened to take my skirt hem from mid-calf to somewhere around my neck, so I gathered as much of it as I could in my fist. At least it was only my thigh flashing the cars jammed into Chicago's traffic.

Another harsh gale whipped strands of my black hair free and some of my skirt out of my grip. While I was pushing the skirt back in place, my purse slipped off my shoulder and landed on the sidewalk. Shifting my eyes from side to side, I checked just how many people might have seen the flash of my tan-colored underwear. My fellow pedestrians weren't paying me any attention.

Thank god.

Bending at the knees, I reached for my navy-and-gold purse. As I stood, my skirt was suddenly rent from my hand, and I found myself trapped in a wind to end all winds.

The breeze cut through my underwear like an ice-cold slap.

I gasped and pushed the fabric down the front of my thighs, but the cold smacked my ass. I moved my hands to the back, but then the front hem snapped against the breast of my jacket. The silky fabric slipped out of my fingers no matter how I struggled to put myself in order.

"Oh shit," a man said from nearby.

With the vortex whistling all around me, I didn't hear his shoes hurry in my direction, but then he was there between me and the line of cars. I was still struggling with my skirt when I felt a completely different type of fabric slip around my thighs. I took in the freckle-dotted knuckles holding a gray suit coat on both sides of my thighs at each lapel. I followed the crisp white sleeves wrapped around strong arms to broad shoulders. Further up was a square jaw with a dusting of auburn beard, lips quirked in a lopsided smile, more freckles on high cheekbones, and tousled auburn hair. Under his thick, straight eyebrows, his copper-colored eyes were apologetic.

He'd blocked me from the wind and covered me. I was shielded and encased by a total stranger, whose thumbs pressed into the naked skin of my upper thigh.

"I just wanted to be a tulip," I whispered to myself.

"Excuse me?" he asked with a soft hint of an Irish accent.

I shook my head, which was only inches from his very attractive face. Attractive or not, he was still a stranger.

His Adam's apple bobbed as he swallowed. "I'm sorry. I just reacted... and now I feel I may have crossed the line."

"Because your hands are under my skirt?"

"When you put it that way, yes."

"Well, thank you for your help, but my clothing seems to be under control now."

Carefully removing his jacket from around my ass, he took two steps back. "Of course."

This time when the wind took my skirt again, I was ready and able to keep it in place. "Honestly, thank you. I was not getting it under control on my own."

He smirked down at the sidewalk, then shifted his eyes to meet mine. The blood started rushing in my ears again, for a completely different reason.

"I'm Daire, by the way," he said.

"Serena. Nice to meet you."

"You as well." The wind forced ripples through his white button-up shirt, revealing the smooth planes of his abs and his rounded pecs.

I bit my lip and forced my eyes back on his. He arched an eyebrow, and I had to smile at him.

"Anyway... have a nice day." His eyes flicked over my face once before he took another step backward.

I could say something polite—wish him a good day as well—but he was easily the most handsome man I'd ever seen. A handsome man, who could fix a problem on his toes, and still respect a woman's need for physical space to feel safe. I *could* say something polite, but I wasn't a fool and let him just walk away.

"I bet your girlfriend really appreciates your quick reflexes," I quipped.

His face lit up with a smile like the sun reflecting off of the lake—almost too bright to look at. "No girlfriend—or boyfriend for that matter."

Taking a step closer to him, I said, "You really were so gallant."

"Knight in shining armor."

"I'm not normally a damsel in distress."

"What are you normally, then?"

"A bit of a badass, actually."

He took a step closer, leaving about a foot between us. "That's more my speed."

My stomach flipped at the way his voice dipped lower.

"What about you? What are you when you're not saving badass women in the streets?" I asked.

He shrugged his broad shoulders. "Irish."

I giggled—honest-to-god giggled. I would have been embarrassed if I wasn't so beguiled by him. "What brings you to the US?"

"I've been here since college."

"They don't have colleges in Ireland?"

"No, they have universities."

I rolled my eyes. "Cute."

His laugh was warm and rumbling. "Ireland just wasn't big enough for me and—I needed somewhere bigger."

I tilted my head to consider him, and he stared right back. "Well, thank you again. I should go, or I'm going to be late for work."

"Me too."

I started on my way again but stopped when he called, "I'd love to hear more about your badassery. Can I take you to dinner?"

I smothered my eagerness as best as I could before turning to face him. "Right to dinner? You don't want my number first?"

"Well, I'll need that to set up the dinner."

I bit my lower lip. "Is this the way you manufacture dates? Wardrobe malfunctions and mysterious comments about Ireland?"

"I've got a skill for spotting a chance and not letting it pass me by. So, can I have your number?"

I nodded.

He pulled his phone from his pocket. I gave him my number, and he sent me a text standing right there on the sidewalk with the wind whipping around us as if it was as excited by this man as I was.

"It'll be nice to get to know you, Daire."

"I'm looking forward to it, Tulip."

He slipped his arms back into his jacket and stepped backward before turning around and continuing on his way. The lines of his suit accentuated his broad athletic frame. He looked back over his shoulder, and even at a distance, his crooked smile made my heart skip a beat.

I practically floated across the street and the rest of the walk to my building. Robin's egg blue skirt didn't seem like the wrong choice anymore.

The sun shone through the wall of windows as I entered the office of Garcia Public Relations LLC. I usually strode in with the professionalism expected of a partner, but my giddiness from meeting Daire just couldn't be tamped down today.

I waved to our front desk administrator Michael. He waved back while continuing his phone call.

The office I shared with Willow, my best friend and fellow partner, was empty. Together we managed the publicists—she was in charge of hiring and training, while I focused on operations and assignments.

My skirt brushed my calves as I swayed past our open door and stopped at the accounting department. "Miya, you coming?"

"I'll be right there," she said with her back to me. The light from her computer screen caught the edges of her tight curls and gave her the illusion of tiny gems adorning her Afro. She must have been involved in a spreadsheet or something because only numbers ever distracted her from meeting a person's eyes.

I raised an eyebrow at Josh, her mentee. "She's in it, huh?"

He spun in his office chair, lacing his fingers behind his head. "Yeah, she's been like that since I got here. Hasn't even touched her coffee."

I gasped melodramatically.

"I'm sorry, have I neglected you?" Miya didn't look up, and her fingers didn't slow on the ten-key.

Josh and I shared a look full of affection for our friend.

When I joined this little PR firm eight years ago, right out of college, I hadn't expected to become so close with all of my coworkers. I thought I would get some work experience and move on to a larger company, but as Garcia Public Relations grew, my name grew with it. And so did my connection to it. I'd somehow devoted a significant chunk of my adult life to this business, and I didn't have any regrets about that.

"No, you have not neglected anyone," I told her. "I'm going to get to the meeting, which starts in"—I checked my watch—"five minutes."

"I'll be there," she said absently.

"I'll catch you later, Josh."

"See ya, Rena."

As I was leaving, I heard Miya say, "Josh, will you set a four-minute timer?"

I was still smiling as I practically swirled into the conference room five minutes later. The warm reddish browns of the table and chairs contrasted with the blues of the walls and the skyline view out of the large windows. Willow sat waiting. Her light brown hair hung in loose curls around her shoulders without their normal uniformity; clearly, the wind had run its fingers through them. She was in her usual seat, and a coffee cup was steaming on the long table in front of my spot next to her.

"Good morning," I said, floating into my chair.

She grinned. "Well, hello. Don't you look cute today." Looking down at her very stylish and professional pencil skirt and blazer, she pouted. "I wish I looked cute."

"Okay, but you weren't the one with your skirt around your shoulders and your underwear flashing all of Chicago."

"No!"

"Yes."

"Oh shit. Are you okay?"

A slow smile spread across my face, and I nodded. "I'm great. Did I say thank you for the coffee?"

Tilting her head, she narrowed her blue eyes at me. "No... but you're welcome. You don't seem upset for someone who could have been arrested for indecent exposure."

"I have underwear on. I couldn't be arrested."

"Not the point. What's going on?"

I leaned forward to explain when loud laughter from the hall cut me off. Willow and I turned to see Miya and Lexi, the head of legal, enter the room. The four of us had been hired within months of each other, and we'd all made partner at the same time when the company began expanding too fast for our boss, Louisa Garcia, to manage on her own.

Lexi and Miya were also dressed in jewel tones and soft fabrics.

Willow sank back in her chair. "Dang it! You all look so cute."

Miya's full lips quirked. "Sorry?" She lowered herself into a seat on the opposite side of the table, the pink of her dress complemented the rosy hues in her dark skin.

"Don't mind me, I'm just the most boring person in the office."

"Not true." Lexi sank into the seat across from Willow. "I think Dirtbag Brad is here today."

"Don't call him names, please. He's a good one," Miya said gently. She was the only one of us who still had the patience to argue with Lexi about her dislike of Bradford Castle, whom everyone else called Ford. Lexi preferred "Brad" probably because of the annoyed look he got every time she did.

"You think everyone is good, Miya."

"Is it slander for you to call our private investigator a dirtbag?" I asked.

"He's not suffering any loss of income from it, and he could just not be a dirtbag."

"I bet it's harassment." Willow turned to Lexi. "Is it harassment?"

Lexi pinched her lips in a tight line. "If I was my legal counsel, I would advise against it. Happy?"

Willow smirked. "Yeah."

"You're lucky Brad's here, or *you'd* be the most *annoying* person in the office."

Miya and I tossed our heads back and laughed, but Willow turned toward me in her chair. "Speaking of annoying, tell me what happened this morning."

"How is that annoying?" I asked.

"It's annoying that you haven't told me yet."

It was almost 9:15 and our meeting would begin shortly. "I'll tell you after."

"Louisa's assistant texted to say she's running late. So, what's going on?" Lexi held up her phone as if its black screen was proof of the text.

Sitting forward, I crossed my arms on the tabletop. "I met someone."

"This morning?" Miya asked.

"I thought you flashed Chicago." A crease formed between Willow's eyebrows.

"How does one flash Chicago?" Lexi pondered.

"I'm wearing a flowy skirt," I answered.

Miya and Lexi looked confused.

"It's so windy," Willow whispered.

Miya gasped. "Oh no, babe, are you okay?"

"Yeah. A very attractive Irishman came to my rescue. He wrapped his suit coat around me, and then we started flirting and we're gonna get dinner."

"An Irishman?" Willow's mouth hung open.

"That's like something out of an old movie." Miya's lips were turned up in a grin. She loved Hollywood classics. Miya had a head for numbers and also for romance.

"Right?" I grinned.

"What's his name?" Lexi tossed her golden hair over her shoulder.

"Daire. I don't know his last name yet."

At my side, Willow chewed on her lower lip.

"You don't know his last name? Okay, you're going to tell us when and where this date is, and we'll just happen to go there at the same time," Lexi said.

I reached across the table to squeeze her hand. It was small in mine, but her petite stature did not diminish her protectiveness over the rest of us. "Obviously."

"Tell us about him." Miya crossed her legs and leaned closer.

"Actually..." Willow started, but I was already saying, "I pretty much told you everything I know. He's somewhere around six feet tall, has, like, the most beautiful auburn hair, and rescues women from public embarrassment."

Lexi narrowed her eyes. "We're definitely coming along on that dinner."

Willow shifted closer to me. "Rena, I can see how excited you are, but—"

"—no issue at all. Chicago is a big city and it's easy to get turned around." Louisa Garcia's voice in the hallway carried through the open door and into the room.

"Shit." Willow grimaced.

I looked over my shoulder to see our boss lead the way into the conference room, with a man in a well-fitted gray suit in tow.

"Thank you for being so understanding," he said with the slightest lilt of an Irish accent.

Oh shit.

"I'm sorry," Willow whispered. It was clear that she'd been trying to warn me. She would have performed his interview and hiring.

His posture was straight and confident as he stood next to Louisa. The smiles fell off of my friends' faces as they looked from the handsome, tall, auburn-haired man to me. His gaze followed theirs and landed on me. There was a light of surprise in his eyes, and then his shoulders sank the smallest amount.

To anyone who didn't know Louisa, she'd seem oblivious to the mood of the room, but she was acutely observant—she scanned the four of us before landing on me as the most likely issue.

I sighed, and she nodded.

We'd talk later.

Brightly, she announced, "Ladies, this is our newest publicist, Daire O'Dowd."

I met his eyes, and even through his warm smile, I swore I could see a reflection of my disappointment. It appeared he was mentally canceling our date as well.

The skirt *was* a bad choice.

Chapter Two

♥

Daire

I entered the conference room and felt an off-putting déjà-vu. Serena sat in the same chair as the first time I'd seen her here. That was where the similarities ended though. Instead of all my managers occupying the space, it was just her. Instead of the soft colors she'd worn a month ago, she wore dark gray slacks and a top the color of merlot. It fit all the way to her neck, but the silky fabric followed the curves of her breasts—a detail I should *not* notice. And it looked like a scene I'd conjured up only a few nights before when I was alone in my bed.

She looked up. Her green eyes flicked down my body and back to my face. Her chest rose and pressed against her shirt, the fabric straining before she exhaled. A detail I *definitely* should not notice.

I flashed her a smile I shouldn't give. It was polite enough, just with a lecherous edge.

She licked her lower lip and grinned back at me.

When we realized we'd be working together, we agreed we couldn't date. She couldn't appear to show favoritism with my client assignments. It was disappointing but fine. But the more I got to know her, the more I saw how her mind worked—and the more I understood the movements of her body. The balance shifted from disappointing to almost devastating. That's how she was—devastatingly clever and beautiful and funny. And out of my reach.

"Hello, Serena." I unbuttoned my suit coat and lowered into the seat across from her.

"Hi, Daire." She rested her elbow on the table, her chin cupped in her palm with her face tilted to look at me through her eyelashes.

It was the first time we'd been in the same room without another person present. The first time I'd had her full attention since meeting on that sidewalk.

"Thank you for coming," she said.

"Thank you for making the time," I replied.

"Of course. Willow will be here soon, and we'll get started then."

It was a simple progress conversation after my first couple of weeks as their employee. I had a few questions about operations, but otherwise, I felt confident in my performance. I enjoyed working there. My coworkers were friendly and helpful—the atmosphere was much more generous than in other PR firms I'd worked at. But it still didn't satisfy my desire to make a difference in the world. I'd always been a person of high ideals, but I'd always needed to pay my bills too. It was really starting to scrape away at me. When I graduated from university, I'd chosen corporate jobs at places that paid more than non-profit organizations could so I could pay down my student loans. But I was getting closer to being able to afford to realign with my values. My position at Garcia Public Relations was facilitating things more amply than I'd even expected.

I leaned forward in my chair. "I heard you and Will get a shot at Hutchington Enterprises."

"We do." She sat straighter in her chair, her shoulders back. "It'd be a big client."

"I hear Gary Hutchington is a bit of a character."

"Me too… He's actually taking a really weird process."

"What does that mean?"

She chewed her lips between her teeth for a moment. "You know how it's normally a meeting and you pitch ideas, and then the client decides?"

"Yeah."

"He's doing a cocktail party, then he'll invite *finalists* back for a face-to-face meeting."

"That is strange."

"So, there's going to be this event full of publicists, and we have to find a way to stand out."

I withheld my cynical comment about Hutchington being able to afford to force people to be his friend.

Instead, I considered her bright green eyes, and dark hair swooped into a sophisticated bun on her head. I couldn't imagine how she could possibly fade into a crowd. I wanted to tell her, but I withheld that too. "Any plans so far?"

She shrugged. "Just say the right thing at the right time."

Hutchington would be a huge get. A career-making client. I'd be happy for her if she brought him in, but I was glad that I wouldn't have to work with him. He'd taken his family money and built a wildly successful real estate business, but he had a history of refusing to pay contractors, exploiting landowners, and violating environmental regulations. He seemed like a real twat. Not that it was my place to hand-pick whom the firm worked for, it wasn't even my place to hand-pick whom I worked for. But it did twist my stomach, and conjure my dad's venomous voice: *You'll sell those high ideals of yours to the highest bidder.*

I forced my jaw to relax. I tended to tighten it at just the thought of my dad.

Serena's eyebrows pinched together.

My smile spread instinctively, hoping to put her back at ease. "You're good at the right thing at the right time."

"What makes you say that?"

"You had me eating out of the palm of your hand within minutes of meeting you."

The apples of her cheeks turned pink. "I think pulling a Marilyn Monroe at the party would definitely make me stand out."

"It *was* unforgettable."

Our eyes locked. In the emerald depths of her gaze lay suppressed heat. An itch unscratched. I recognized a mirror of what lay just below the surface in me as well. A growing need for her—a whisper becoming a shout.

"Sorry I'm late," Willow said breezing through the open conference room and popping the tension in the room like a balloon. "I had to deal with a Twitter emergency. Did you two get started?"

"No, we waited for you." Serena looked down at the sheets of paper on the table in front of her.

"Everything okay on Twitter?" I asked Willow purposefully not watching the way Serena flicked her fingertips over her tongue.

"Is anything ever okay on Twitter?" Willow rolled her blue eyes.

I chuckled.

"Anyway," she continued, taking a seat next to Serena, "how have you been doing? You seem to be settling in well."

It was nearing the end of the workday, hours after my meeting with Willow and Serena, but I still stared at my computer screen wondering if I was making something out of nothing with Serena. Yes, when we'd first met on the sidewalk our chemistry had been instantaneous. I was attracted to her, and she seemed to be attracted to me, but that didn't mean anything really. Attraction ebbed and flowed, as did crushes.

The pull she had over me was real—I could sense her in any room—but there was no reason to think it was more than one-sided.

"Daire, I cannot watch that poor little cactus slowly die any longer," Quinn said from his desk to my left pulling me from my thoughts and back into the office I shared with him and Latasha.

I raised my eyebrows. "I'm sorry?"

"That poor thing needs light. I'm gonna put it on the sill in the conference room." Standing, he grabbed the little potted plant and strode out our open door.

To my right, Latasha shook her head, her hoop earrings swaying with the motion.

"Plant guy?" I asked.

Her dark brown eyes held only affection for our coworker. "He can't help caring too much about everything."

I understood her meaning. Quinn was not only the first to offer me help to settle into my responsibilities, but he'd also coordinated an after-work birthday party for Josh in account-ing the Friday before last.

"That's..."

I considered my next word, but she supplied, "Precious, right?"

A smile split across my face. "It is kind of precious."

Quinn walked back into our office and sighed. The tension relaxed from his shoulders. "That's better. The little guy will survive there."

"Thank god you were here," Latasha deadpanned.

He nodded in mock grave agreement. "I know, it was the nick of time."

"I didn't even realize it was dying." I swiveled to face my computer again.

There was a pause before he said, "We don't have windows in our office."

I gave a lopsided shrug, before looking over my shoulder. "Honestly, it was so green when I bought it I thought it was fake."

They both threw their heads back and laughed, and I joined in. Sharing a space with them wasn't a hardship, even when Latasha hummed off-key to her music and Quinn mumbled to himself through his thoughts. Our office was a decent-sized room but filled to capacity with three small desks pressed against the walls.

All in all, it was an easy workplace... and I still wasn't satisfied.

I finished up the last of my work for the day and locked my computer. Most of my coworkers left themselves logged in, but it made me feel vulnerable. For the rest of the day, Quinn told everyone walking by about the cactus' near-death experience and my not being able to tell the difference between a live plant and a fake one. Each time, Latasha shook her head and smiled, and I laughed along as the butt of the joke.

The office was mostly empty as I strode down the quiet hall. I paused at the doorway of the accounting department, where Josh was still typing away.

"Hey," I said, leaning against the jam.

He startled, and swiveled in his seat, his hand pressed to his chest. "Shit, you scared me."

"Sorry, I was just heading out. I think we're the last ones here. Do you want me to switch off the lights, or are you about to leave?"

"No, I'm good. I was just finishing up. I'll come with you." He turned off his monitor as he stood.

"You don't need more time?"

"Nah."

Josh talked about a Crossfit class he was going to be late for as we walked together. The man was built like a house, broader and taller than me. We turned a corner and the suite's main entrance came into view, as well as Serena's swaying hips. Her slacks clung to the top curve of her ass and then hung straight all the way down her legs. And yet another thing I shouldn't notice.

"Hey, Rena," Josh called, his grin wide.

"Hi, guys." She held the door open for us to walk through, and turned off the lights with a swipe of her hand. "How was your day?"

"You know, a day," he answered.

"Good, thank you. How was yours?" I asked, keeping my attention toward her polite.

"Productive."

I stood between her and Josh as we waited for the elevator. It was less than a minute for it to reach our level. Standing that close to Serena, I could smell her herbal scent. The one that had swirled around us when the wind had swept me into her orbit.

There was a ding, and then the stainless-steel doors slid open, and I held my hand out for Serena to enter first. She pushed the button for the lobby and leaned against the adjacent wall. Josh followed her, taking the back wall leaving me to lean against the wall opposite her.

The doors began to close.

I couldn't think of anything to say except small talk or outright flirtation.

I waited for Josh to start talking—he was a chatty guy—but just before the doors closed fully, he shot his hand between them. "Shit, I forgot something." The opening expanded, and he twisted sideways to squeeze back into the hallway.

"Everything okay?" Serena asked.

"Yeah, I just forgot my gym bag. I'll see you guys tomorrow."

"See you tomorrow."

"Have a good night." I lifted my hand in a wave.

Looking across the elevator car, I found Serena looking back at me. Instantly, the charge I'd felt when I'd first met her and for the brief moment we were alone earlier today sizzled in the air between us. I could practically hear it in my ears, sparking under my skin. A tug drew me to close the space between us. I gripped the railing on both sides of my hips and stayed where I was.

She pushed the button to close the doors again. Trapping us. Alone.

The silence stretched and layered, growing thick.

"How was your day?" I asked, needing to say something anything, to fill the space. Then I remembered. "Productive. You already said that."

Her lips lifted in a lopsided smirk. "Yeah, and yours was 'Good, thank you.'"

I smiled back. "Nice of you to remember."

"It was unforgettable," she practically whispered.

The pull she had on me tightened, and I stood straight with my hands still clinging to the railing.

She swallowed again. "I heard about your cactus."

"Of course you did."

"It was reassuring proof that you're human, and capable of mistakes." Her voice was low. I leaned toward her, hungry for every word.

"Oh, I'm very human. And I'm contemplating a couple of mistakes as we speak."

It wasn't until she shifted toward me that I realized I'd taken a step closer. We were both startled when a ding announced the end of our descent, and the doors slid open on the ground floor. I stood in the middle of the car as sunlight lit the distance between us. Now that our shadows were cast against the back wall, I could see just how close I'd come to making those mistakes. Serena blinked as if she exited a trance.

"Oh my god," she muttered to herself.

I ran a hand through my hair and backed away from her. "I'm sorry, Tulip—" I shook my head at the nickname my mind wouldn't forget. "Serena. That will not happen again."

"No, it won't," she agreed. "I will do a better job maintaining... a professional distance."

"Of course." I moved out of her way, so she could exit. I contemplated riding the elevator up, but the cowardice didn't sit well. Instead, I followed her out the building's front door.

A professional distance was the right thing to do, but despite my humiliation at my behavior and her rejection, I knew that if we ever let ourselves give in to our attraction, there would be something deeper underneath. Something that would fit against my jagged edges and smooth them. I had only my intuition to go on, but I would have bet everything I had on it.

Chapter Three

♥

Serena

It had been two months since I'd ridden the elevator alone with Daire, and the memory still made me cringe. But I had kept that professional distance, just as I'd promised.

Unfortunately, that didn't stop me from liking him. He had an ease and charisma about him, like the air around him was energized. Everyone leaned a little closer to hear him talk, but he was quick to find a common interest with people and share the spotlight. In three short months, he'd proven himself to be an asset to the firm. We usually worked in pairs, but he didn't have a set partner. Instead, he dropped in wherever needed.

I suffered from an all-consuming infatuation, and the only way I knew how to protect myself from it was to avoid him. We spoke about work and nothing else. And only when another person was present.

So, when Willow limped into our office on a Monday afternoon with a crutch tucked into one armpit and proclaimed, "I'm grounded," I knew exactly what that meant for me and Daire.

"Oh, Will, no."

We had known it was unlikely she'd be allowed to fly, so we had a backup plan in place.

Her desk was on the other side of the room, but she leaned her hip against mine. Her lower lip pushed out in a pout as she glared down at the green cast around her left leg—an injury she'd gotten when an SUV ran a red light and careened into the driver's side of her car.

She squeezed her hands into fists. "I know. I can't believe it. I'm so disappointed. My doctor said that my leg could swell too much on the flight and the cast might have to be cut off. So, I have to wait for the removable cast."

"I'm sorry, buddy."

She scratched at the top of the plaster through her skirt, a few inches above her knee, and groaned. "It itches so badly."

"You okay?"

"I'm just so disappointed," she said. "I want to bring Hutchington in with you."

"I know."

She pushed up from my desk. "I should put my leg up. It's like all the blood in my body is inside this cast."

"Do you need me to get you anything?"

"No, but thanks anyway. I'm just getting anxious. You know I get this way when I'm not active. It's only been a couple of days, but it's already catching up with me."

Willow was one of the more athletic people I knew. She participated in intramural sports, swam, hiked, and was generally outdoorsy. She ran a marathon last summer. It was hard to imagine how she would fill her time without those things.

I had an inkling of concern about how she was taking the accident emotionally, but every time I asked, she assured me that there was nothing to worry about.

"I'll drop off some books," I offered.

She sat, and guided her leg onto the stool next to her. "Don't worry about it. Miya already did. She also left me with a bunch of watercolors and colored pencils and coloring books."

"Well... I guess I'll bring you a 3D puzzle or something."

"Thank you, but you really don't have to."

"Oh no, I'm going to. I'll make sure it's wildly inappropriate, like a picture of a butt plug or something."

Her cackle laugh bounced off of the wall of windows. "You think they make butt plug 3D puzzles?"

"It's gonna be an interesting Google search."

By the time we stopped laughing, my stomach hurt and she'd wiped her fingertips under her eyes.

I opened my mouth to ask her how the rest of her doctor's appointment had gone when the pull in the room shifted. I knew before I looked.

Daire was in our open doorway.

He knocked two knuckles on the door jamb. "I'm sorry to disturb you."

He gave me a perfunctory head nod, and I returned it. I pointedly did not look at how the sunlight through the window glinted in the vibrant colors of his hair. Or how the stark lines of his navy suit elongated his frame.

It was best not to look at him at all. One look wanted two; two wanted four.

He was a very lookable man.

And completely off-limits.

Even if at the end of my long workdays, it was his copper eyes I imagined looking up at me from just below my pelvis.

Willow waved him in. "No disturbance, at all."

"I got your email." He jerked his head in my direction, then to Willow he said, "So no flying for you?"

I knew it had to be him replacing her, but to have it actually happening was... complex. On one hand, I couldn't think of a more adaptable person to step in for her. On the other hand, the distance I maintained from him was the only thing keeping me from ripping my clothes off in his presence. And in this scenario, I had three hands, because, on the third one, there was the tiniest flutter blooming inside of me. A dangerous flutter.

A flutter that did not abide by *professional distance*.

"Yup. I'm homebound." Willow squinted at the ceiling. "Or bound to my home or something. I don't know."

"May I?" He gestured to the russet-colored sofa across from the window displaying Chicago's summer skyline.

"Of course."

Unbuttoning his jacket with one hand, he sat. He crossed his ankle over his knee and draped one arm across the back of the sofa. The image he made was captivating.

I made myself look away.

Very lookable man.

"So, let's get me up to speed on Hutchington," he said.

I explained to Daire the plan for the trip in two days that Willow was no longer able to join me on. One of those days would be partially taken up with a flight to northern California. Then a dinner party hosted by Hutchington, the following night. If everything went well, we'd hopefully be invited for a one-on-one meeting with him to further discuss the firm's services, as if the event was an episode of *The Bachelor*.

Acquiring this client would push Garcia Public Relations into the rink with bigger, more prestigious PR firms, and solidify our reputation.

I needed to focus, but my biggest distraction would be with me every step of the way.

A few hours later, Daire stretched his arms over his head and stood. He'd long since abandoned his suit coat, now tossed over the sofa arm. The breath had caught in my throat as he undid the button at his sleeve and rolled his white shirt up to his elbows, before repeating the process on the other side. After that, focusing on my work was an exercise in futility. Instead, I participated in a new kind of torture, pretending not to see the fine muscles in his forearms.

"It'll be hard to fill your shoes," he said to Willow, leaning over to grab his jacket.

"You'll have Rena with you. You'll do great." She scratched her thigh.

"Itches? I had a cast on my arm when I was a lad. When they opened it up, they found all the pencils I'd lost in there."

She scrunched her nose. "There's already one in there somewhere."

He chuckled and shook his head. "How long ya got the cast?"

"Six to eight weeks."

"That fuckin' sucks."

She shrugged. "It really does."

"Well, I'll get out of your hair. Thanks for your help on all this. Have a good nigh'."

It was a terrible idea, but I watched him leave the room. He carried his jacket hooked on his finger over his shoulder. His white shirt hugged his shoulders and shifted at his waist with every stride. Just before he turned the corner, he looked back and met my eyes. All of the air was forced out of my lungs, my insides rearranged. His step faltered for just a moment, then he was blocked from my view.

I looked across the room to find Willow shaking her head at me.

She glanced into the hallway and then back to me. "You two have... chemistry..."

I swallowed, still reeling. "It's fine. He's a professional. I'm a professional. We'll get our jobs done. It'll be fine."

"You're not even going to miss me, are you?"

I gasped. "Of course I will! Why would you say that?"

"Because you get to travel with the object of your lust."

I hadn't wanted to tell her how inappropriate my feelings were for him, but I'd needed help with the whole never being alone with him thing—which was really shot to shit now.

My black braid swung down my back, as I looked out our door into the quiet hallway. "Shut up! And don't say it like that. It makes him sound like a dildo."

She lifted a dark eyebrow.

"Oh my god!"

Rolling her eyes, she shrugged. With her focus on her computer, I went back to my work as well. A few minutes later both of our emails dinged. I opened mine and read Lexi's cryptic message.

Please come to the conference room at 5:30 p.m.

"That's weird," Willow muttered.

Most of the offices Willow and I passed on the way to the conference room were empty, including the one Daire shared with Latasha and Quinn. I glanced through the open door at his clean workspace. There was also a photo, but I couldn't make it out as I passed—even moving slowly to stay in pace with Willow.

In the conference room, Lexi stood near Louisa's shoulder at the head of the table, and Miya sat on her usual side with her back to the windows. Instantly, it was clear that there was something wrong. There was a deep crease between Lexi's pale eyebrows. Miya's shoulders hunched, and she gave us the smallest welcoming smile. It was hard to place what was off about Louisa—almost as if she was too precisely in order, too unruffled.

"Willow, Serena, thank you for joining us," she said, standing and gesturing to our usual chairs.

Something large loomed in the corner of the room, and I turned to see Ford, our firm's private investigator.

His thick, dark eyebrows were pulled down by his temples over soft, dark blue eyes. He was a handsome man, if a bit rough around the edges. I'd never seen him in clothes that weren't well-loved. Jeans frayed above his scuffed boots and threadbare T-shirts were his normal uniform. His salt-and-pepper hair was always a little too long with an unruly curl. He was a Carhartt jacket away from fitting in with the guys I grew up with in rural Michigan. His look was probably purposefully curated—just a normal guy going about a normal day, asking normal questions.

"Sorry, Rena," he said.

"As I said earlier, Brad, you should take a seat. No need to lurk." Lexi's tone was a study in professionalism, but it lacked warmth.

The same could be said for his returned smile. "I'm happy to stand."

"Lurker," Willow joked, and he shot her a wink, but it didn't take long for his focus to rest on Lexi. It never took long.

I shared a knowing look with Willow as I slid into my seat, and she literally fell into hers.

"Your leg bothering you?" Miya asked.

Willow nodded. "Yeah, I'm okay though. I'll just have to rest after this."

"Ladies, we have unfortunate news," Louisa said, pulling all eyes to her. "I'm going to cut straight to it. We have evidence that someone is embezzling from the company."

I replayed her words in my head, ensuring that I'd heard her correctly.

"What?" Willow demanded.

Louisa nodded. "A couple of days ago, Miya found a false consulting account that we paid a couple of thousand dollars to."

I looked across the table at Miya. She looked so alone—lost in her thoughts. I wanted to reach across the table and grab her hand, ask her if she was okay. Miya prided herself on being meticulous with her work. It must have been terrible for her to find the account, to search through the numbers and realize they didn't lead where they were supposed to.

"It appears the payment was made almost three months ago," Louisa continued. "Then Miya found a second one done shortly after the first, and a third one a week ago. All three transactions were done from different employee numbers. We do not know who the guilty party is."

I didn't bother asking if they'd spoken to the police. They couldn't. The optics would devastate our business. It would be used against us in every pitch, and our competitors would use it to poach our clients.

It'd capsize us.

"Because you all leave your computers unlocked, it'd be easy to file an expense with everything out in the open," Ford said from behind me.

Lexi's lips pinched in distaste.

He ignored her. "There are probably even more transactions."

Miya sank a few inches in her seat. "I know there must be. I'll find them."

I lowered the hand I hadn't realized was over my mouth. "I had no idea."

She ran her hands over her thighs under the tabletop. "There wasn't any need for you to know."

My eyebrows pulled together. "But there is now?"

Her dark curly hair haloed her round cheeks. The effect caused her already sympathetic eyes and gentle face to take on an angelic quality.

"How well do you know Daire O'Dowd?" Ford asked me.

Training alone forced my face to neutral, while confusion roiled under the surface. "Why do you ask?"

"Three months..." Willow whispered next to me.

I sucked in a deep breath. "You think it's Daire?"

Lexi held up a hand. "We don't know."

"Were any of the transactions on his computer?" I asked.

"Not his." Ford crossed his arms over his chest. "But from both of his deskmates. He is also one of the few of you that actually locks his computer."

"I will send a memo, reminding everyone to lock their computers from now on," Lexi bit out.

"Thank you. That will help in the *future*," he deadpanned.

"Have you seen anything suspicious with Daire?" I asked, knowing that if I was hearing this, he had already had a peek through Daire's files.

"No, but if he's smart, I wouldn't."

"We do not *know* who is responsible. There's"—Lexi paused, clearly considering her words—"reason to believe that it *could* be Daire. But we are not making accusations."

"That being said, you're about to go on a trip with him, right?" Ford asked me, clearly already knowing the answer.

"Yes?"

"We need you to keep an eye on him." Louisa's leveled tone broke through the frantic energy that was building around us. "Make him comfortable, see if he says anything."

My mouth hung open.

"She's a publicist, not a spy. What are you expecting her to do?" Willow narrowed her eyes at our boss.

"I don't expect anything, but if he says something, I want her to know what she's looking for."

"Do you actually think it's Daire?" I asked the room.

Ford shrugged his broad shoulders.

Miya spoke up, "I think whoever it is, we know them. We're friends with them. We care about their lives. On the other end of this crime, is someone we *care* about."

"Your kindness is commendable as always, but whoever this is could ruin everything we've built." Louisa met my eyes. "We need to find them. We need to do it quickly, but more importantly, we need to do it quietly."

I swallowed and looked up at Ford. "How do I do this?"

Chapter Four

♥

Serena

By the time I arrived at O'Hare for my flight, I'd had a day and a half to process the broader scope that someone was embezzling money from the firm, but I hadn't come to terms with the suspicion that it could be Daire. Just as there wasn't any evidence to prove that he stole the money, there wasn't any evidence to prove otherwise.

All I really had to go off of was Ford's direction. "Have your eyes open. If he does or says something suspicious, take note of it. Nothing else. Don't try to get information out of him. Just pay attention."

I'd nodded, and he'd bent at the waist to meet my eye. "Rena, I'm serious. Don't try to pry information out of him. We don't know what he's capable of."

"Jesus Christ," Willow had said angrily. "If she's unsafe, she can't go."

"We have no evidence to suspect Daire, and there is no reason to believe Serena is in any danger," Lexi had argued.

Willow had opened her mouth again, but I'd cut her off. "It's not Daire, and I'll be just fine." Ford had opened his mouth, but I'd cut him off too. "I will pay attention and be careful, and nothing else."

No one seemed satisfied, but in the end, Daire and I were still going on this trip.

I spotted him instantly, like he was due north and my eyes would always land on him. He sat in a blue vinyl chair at our gate, wearing a dark green button-up, the top button undone. I'd only ever seen him in a suit and tie at the office. Now I could see the little dip at the bottom of his neck between his collarbones.

One of his ankles rested on the knee of his other leg. Light gray slacks I recognized from the office took on a more casual appearance in this setting.

He looked up from the paperback book he held open with one long-fingered hand.

I gave him a warmer-than-usual smile.

A muscle flexed in his sharp jaw.

"Good mornin'." He nodded and went back to his reading.

Maybe he wasn't a morning person. Maybe he just wanted to read. Or maybe he still saw me for what I was, his boss.

Or... maybe he was stealing money from our work.

Nothing had changed about whether or not I was a spy—I wasn't one. But I was acutely skilled at reading social dynamics and strategies.

I lowered into the seat across from him and opened my phone to the e-book I was reading last. Mimicking his body language, I draped my ankle over my knee. "What are you reading?"

He glanced up at me under his brow and lifted the book to reveal the cover of a science fiction novel. "Are you reading?"

I nodded, then looked down to read the title. I paused when I recalled the last time I'd opened my book app. Alone. In my bed. In need of inspiration that wasn't Daire.

"And what are you reading?" he asked.

My mouth hung open as I tried to remember the title to a classic novel... or *any* novel at all. My mind was blank as heat rose up my neck.

Say something.

"I don't know."

Brilliant.

He chuckled and tilted his head considering me. "You don't know?"

"Nope."

"You can't tap the screen and see the title?"

I tapped the screen. *Shackled by Lust,* I shook my head. "Not one I want to share."

He leaned forward, placing both feet on the floor and resting his elbows on his thighs. With his voice lowered, he asked, "Is it... explicit?"

"Would you be scandalized?"

"Aghast."

Lifting my phone, I started to read. "Then I don't think I should answer that question."

He shifted back in his seat and opened his book again. Over the top of my phone, I saw him grin and shake his head.

On the plane, I hefted my carry-on above me, stretching to put it in the overhead compartment. I was about to lift on my tiptoes when one of his hands braced the suitcase. He wasn't touching me—not his stomach to my back or his thigh against mine—but he was so close. I went stock-still. It was that, or liquefy into a puddle on the floor.

"I've got it." His voice was only inches from my ear.

It took me a second to lower my arms. I glanced over my shoulder, and his mouth was right at eye level, his lips slightly parted. It would be so easy to brush my lips against his.

I wanted to trust him. I wanted him to be everything he seemed to be. But the seed of doubt had been planted. I needed to remember that I really didn't know him. That my instincts were skewed by the heady attraction I felt for him.

Someone shifted behind him, and I realized I was holding up the line.

"Excuse me," I muttered, sliding into the window seat.

My work life had always been my first priority because I liked it. In the past, not dating someone because it would reflect badly on me professionally had never been a struggle. But less than an hour into this trip alone with Daire, and I was already jabbing the holes in those defenses.

Once I got to my hotel room tonight, I'd regain the ground I'd lost. I'd strengthen my resolve. I just had to keep it together until then.

After taking care of his bag, he sat next to me, his broad body and long legs crammed into the middle seat.

"Do you need to switch?" I asked.

"No, I'm fine, thank you."

"Are you sure? You don't fit well there."

"I won't fit well there either."

We fell into what almost felt like easy silence. He spent the entire flight looking over my shoulder at the puffy white clouds under the plane's belly.

Every move he made—unbuttoning a button of his shirt revealing a sliver of white cotton underneath, rolling his sleeves up his forearms, and licking the tip of his finger to turn the page of his book—was erotic in my eyes.

In the stale reused air of the plane, his scent stood out—something that was clean and reminded me of juniper. A trigger to my desire, and a reminder of the day we met, when his scent swirled around us caught in the wind that pressed us together. I had almost convinced myself that most of my memories of that moment were fabricated, that I'd conjured them to be more intense than they actually were, but he smelled exactly as I remembered.

By the time we landed from our four-and-a-half-hour flight, I couldn't think in words, just emotions and sensation and unfulfilled wants.

I wasn't sure how I was going to survive the car ride with just the two of us and that scent that was making me feral, but through some brush of luck, we were assigned a convertible rental. When I'd pushed the button to lower the car top, Daire lifted one ruddy eyebrow but said nothing. The roof folded into place behind the back seat just as it was supposed to, unlike the dashboard screen that refused to light up. After a few minutes of trying, he pulled his phone out of his back pocket and typed in our resort's address.

I sat in the passenger seat, enjoying the brilliant California sun soaking into my skin.

He drove with one elbow resting on the driver's side door, the other gripping the top of the steering wheel as he maneuvered around curving cliff-side roads. The sun set golden rays in his hair. Even though it was unwise, I couldn't deny myself the pleasure of the sight of his strong jaw and full lips outlined by the Pacific Ocean.

At the hotel, he parked as I rolled my suitcase up the ramp, into the front door of the resort with its windows overlooking the waves crashing against jagged rocks. I didn't want to think about how expensive a single room in this place was, let alone two. But it wasn't my job to worry about expenses. It normally wouldn't even be a blip on my radar, but that was before I knew someone was stealing from the firm.

It was my job, and Daire's, to land the client.

It was not my job to prove Daire's guilt or innocence.

But with every new dollar sign attached to the trip, the pressure to do just that increased.

"Hello," a young man greeted me from behind the front counter. His cornrows were in neat, even lines, and his white shirt was pristine against his light brown skin.

"Hi, I should have two rooms booked for Garcia Public Relations," I replied.

He clicked away on his keyboard. After a few too many seconds and watching his face shift into a neutral expression, I sensed there might be an issue.

"They might be under my name Serena Jackson. Or possibly under Daire O'Dowd."

"No, I found the room under the business name."

My relief was quickly replaced with unease as I registered his words. "Room?"

"Yes, miss, I only see one."

My stomach dropped.

"That..." I shook my head. "That can't be possible."

"Unfortunately, everything I check only shows the one."

I could *not* share a room with a man I had been fantasizing about for months. A man I needed to keep my hands off of.

"There must be a mistake. Give me just a moment." I made every effort to appear professional and calm, but in my mind, I sputtered a series of curse words aimed at whoever had made this epic mishap.

My fingers flew over my phone screen typing in the group text with Lexi, Miya, and Willow. ***Why is there only one room???***

What do you mean only one room? Willow replied.

We're here and the hotel only has one room reserved.

The three little dots appeared and disappeared. They came back again. Then Miya texted, ***That's not right. Give me a sec.***

Every second that passed felt like an eternity. I pictured her messaging Josh, whom I assumed was the one who changed the reservation accommodations.

It must have only been a minute or two, but finally, she said, ***The confirmation says two. I'll call.***

Thanks, Miya!

Three dots came and went again. Then Lexi sent, ***So, you may not want to hear this... But maybe this could work out for us. You know...***

I glared down at my phone. ***Too soon. And I thought you weren't pointing any fingers.***

Not cool, Lex, Willow added.

I'm not. You may just as well prove his innocence, you know, Lexi backed off.

Still not cool.

Two feet away from me, the phone behind the counter rang.

"I think that's her," I said to the clerk. "Do you mind answering it?"

"Of course." He reached for the receiver and held it to his ear. "Thank you for calling Cliff Side Resort, Anton speaking, how may I help you... Yes, ma'am, she has arrived."

I tried not to glare as I listened to only his side of the conversation.

"I'm sorry, I just checked, and there are no more," he said.

I forced my fists to loosen—little half-moons pressed into the skin of my palms.

"Unfortunately, for fire safety and insurance reasons, that isn't possible in that room... No, ma'am, I'm sorry a janitor closet cannot be re-purposed... Yes, I am sure."

I closed my eyes as I filled in what I couldn't hear. My toe tapped an urgent beat on the tile floor.

"Yes, ma'am, I can accommodate that... Of course, we'll make their stay as comfortable as possible."

I didn't hear Daire approach, but I felt him. A warm presence that eased my nervous system—which was bad, even if it did feel comforting.

He leaned against the counter to my right. "What's goin' on?"

His voice reached through my current mini-tragedy and pushed the air out of my lungs. That voice *did* things to me. It was deep and rumbling. It hit some corner of my brain directly attached to arousal.

My emotional state needed to pick a lane.

His clean summer scent filled my nose. I looked over my shoulder at him before I could consider if it was wise. Between hearing him and smelling him, I was being bombarded by sensory overload. His face was only inches from mine. My fingers longed to brush through his windswept hair. And his lower lip was full and pouty, so close I could practically feel it against mine. Three out of the five senses of Daire was too much.

"There's only one room." My voice somehow didn't betray any of the riotous sensations he caused.

Reaching into his pocket, he said, "It's fine. I'll pay for a room myself and get reimbursed later."

The clerk hung up the phone and faced us with an apologetic look. "I'm sorry, sir, we don't have any vacancies."

"How did this happen?" I asked.

Anton sighed. "It just looks like an unfortunate mistake."

I bit my lips between my teeth, and Daire swallowed.

"I've already upgraded your stay to our best package," Anton continued. "All of our amenities are open to you, including room service. Ms. Vasquez said you have work to accomplish, so perhaps eating in your room tonight would help save you time."

That earned him a glare from Daire that I kinda wanted to be on the receiving end of. The cheeks reddened under the freckles.

"How many beds?"

Chapter Five

Daire

There was only one.

Only one fuckin' bed.

Fuckin' hell.

The king-sized bed stretched across the floor of our room covered in a white duvet. It was almost too big for the space, with just a thin path around it. Serena stood between me and the bed, and I damn near screamed all of my dirty thoughts out loud just looking at her. Her burgundy top and black slacks clinging to her figure were in sharp contrast against the white of the comforter.

One. Fuckin'. Bed.

She gripped the handle of her navy suitcase with white knuckles. This must be a damn nightmare for her. I couldn't go as far as all of that. When I'd heard that we would be traveling together, this had been my exact fantasy.

Well, not exactly. But it was the beginning of my fantasy.

She was the beginning of all of my fantasies. Her green eyes begging me for more. Her black hair cascading down her naked back. Her breath catching as I sank into her.

Good god in heaven, help me.

I needed to get my thoughts under control, or she would see just how I felt about this arrangement—that it was anything but a hardship for me.

"How's this goin' to work?"

"Well, Daire," she said my name like a challenge, "it's a bed. I assume we'll just sleep in it."

"As long as you're okay with sharing."

"What would you do if I wasn't?"

"It'd be a tight fit in the car, but I could do it."

The hint of a smile ghosted her lips. "Thank you for that. But it's no big deal."

Maybe to you.

Outside the sliding glass door, the sky transitioned from pale blue to pinks and golds over the dark ocean.

"Early nigh' then?" I asked.

"I would like to eat first."

Did she have any idea what she did to me? How her presence pulled at me no matter how I tried to resist her? How often I played back the warmth of her skin against the backs of my thumbs on the day that I'd met her? What would be different between us if I'd walked into a different building and met a different room of managers—one that didn't include her?

Since the night in the elevator, I'd hardly spoken to her alone. Did she think that my interest in her had waned, when it was the exact opposite? Even from the distance I kept, she grew more lovely. More desirable. More engaging.

"Alrigh', food. Then bed?" I followed her further into the room. "Are you a cuddler?"

I wished there was a lever that I could pull to open the floor beneath me and plummet to the center of the earth. I'd asked if she was a *cuddler*. I was already careening down the wrong road if maintaining professional decorum was the goal.

She bit into her voluptuous lower lip. Everything about her was voluptuous. Her tits. Her ass that was fuller than her shoulders were wide. Her goddamn thighs I wanted to be in between so badly.

Her green eyes assessed me. I didn't look away under her scrutiny.

"I am."

One side of my lips curled up.

"But I promise to... not," she went on.

What do I gotta do to get you to promise to do it?

She took a step deeper into the room. My eyes flicked down to the curve of her hip before I could stop myself. Her ass swayed with the glide of her gait.

It was gonna be a long fuckin' night.

Correction—two nights, hopefully, three if we were invited back after the dinner party.

"Would you like to clean up first, or should I?" I nodded toward the closed door that I assumed was the bathroom.

"Do you mind if I go first?"

"I'd be a shithead to offer and then take it back, eh?"

She cocked one hip out. I was always staring at her hips; I'd need to be more discreet. "That *would* be a shithead move. Are you a shithead?"

"No, Tulip, I'm not. Bathroom's all yours."

She just stood there blinking at me, her lips slightly parted. Confused, I thought back on what I'd said.

Tulip. I *was* a shithead.

"Sorry, Serena..."

"I'll just... clean up then."

I nodded and pretended to be very interested in the coastline as she bent over to search through her suitcase.

"Do you mind ordering room service while I'm in there?" she asked.

"Sure, what would you like?"

"Whatever's most expensive." Then she closed herself inside of the bathroom, the lock clicking into place.

Alone, I shook my head and chuckled. I found the menu on the two-person table by the sliding door and ordered the bouillabaisse for her and a Flat Iron steak for myself—the second most expensive item. I hesitated to order it, but it claimed to be grass-fed and ethically raised. And although I'd considered veganism for years because of its environmental friendliness, I still hadn't made that leap.

Then I tried to read my book sitting at the little table, but it only reminded me of the explicit content she was supposedly reading at the airport. What would I learn about her desires if I discovered the book's title? By the time she opened the door, I had to strategically cover where my erection strained against my zipper.

A short while later, I stepped out of the bathroom. I'd changed into the one pair of jeans that I'd packed and a fresh white undershirt.

I spotted her standing on the balcony, the edges of her cardigan whipping in the wind, the curves of her hips clad in dark denim. She looked over her shoulder when I slid the glass door open and stepped out to join her.

Saltwater air mingled with the scent of her, something I couldn't quite place—herbal, softly floral. I liked it. I leaned on the railing next to her and looked out. The last of the sun's rays reached for the stars in the sky.

My eyes flicked to Serena, and the world was made pale by her beauty.

"What are you thinkin' about?" I asked.

She looked back at me and breathed in, her breasts pressed against the neckline of her shirt. "Work."

I gestured to the horizon. "When all of this is here, you're thinkin' about work?"

"We're only here because we have a job to do. Don't judge me."

"I'm not." I held my hands out in defense. "I've grown rather impressed with your mind."

"You have?"

"Of course. You're brilliant."

Her lips pursed and lifted on one side. My gaze lingered a little too long, and I found myself leaning a little closer as she leaned toward me.

The magnetism between us only kept growing stronger with closer proximity.

A knock on the hallway door severed the strings that tied us together, and we snapped apart.

"I'll get it." I pushed off the railing and moved to open the door.

The waiter laid out the food on the table, each plate covered in a silver dome. There was even a single red rose placed in the center, and they'd thrown in a complimentary bottle of prosecco.

"Enjoy your meal," he said as he pushed the cart out of the room and into the hallway.

Serena entered from the balcony and surveyed the table. I reached for the back of her chair and pulled it out before I realized what I was doing. Heat rosied my cheeks—the curse of being red-haired and pale-skinned. "Sorry."

"Is that what you would have done on our date? Pulled out my chair?"

Gesturing to the chair as evidence, I stepped around to my side of the table. "I would have opened your doors too."

She lowered into her seat and scooted closer to the table. "Very chivalrous. But you know I can do all that for myself, right?"

I poured a glass of prosecco and set it in front of her and then did the same for myself, before setting the bottle back in the ice bath. "You do a great many things for yourself. If we're looking at it that way, what could I do for you that you can't do for yourself?" I marked off my points on my fingers. "You have friendships, you seem to enjoy your work, and you provide for yourself."

I set the bottle back in its place and sat in the seat across from her. "It's not about doing something that you can't do for yourself, it's about *doing* something for *you*."

"Does it make you uncomfortable that I can take care of myself?"

"No."

"Then why are you single?"

I ran the tip of my tongue back and forth on one of my canines, searching for some way to skate around the truth. The voice of my father whispered, *No one could love you*. A voice I struggled to ignore. Finally, I said, "Uh... I don't know how to answer that. Why are *you* single?"

"Because in my experience, men want me to need them."

She sat with her back straight and her chin up, but there was a tenderness in her green eyes that spoke of vulnerability. I fisted my hand in my lap to keep from gripping her hand in mine.

I was still searching for a way to respond when she shrugged. "But you know, you're right. What do I need them for?"

With a couple of things in the works, I hoped I could convince her to reconsider that fact. If our roles were different.

She lifted the silver lid off of her plate, and her shoulders fell. "Oh no."

"What's wrong?"

"There's scallops in this."

"Do you not like them?"

"I think I might be allergic because they make my mouth go numb."

"Oh, well you migh' be." I reached across the table and switched her plate with mine.

"No, it's my fault, I should have realized. All I said was the most expensive item."

"Well, you'll have to settle for the second most expensive."

She reached toward the plate in front of me. "Daire, it's fine. I'll just order something else."

Without thinking, I pressed my fingers to the back of her hand. Her eyes snapped to mine. I held completely still. If I moved at all I might do something stupid like stroke my thumb along the pads of her fingers.

"Enjoy the steak." I pulled my hand away, already missing her warmth.

Throughout dinner, we talked about Hutchington's cocktail party/meeting and formulated a strategy that played to our respective strengths. There were fleeting glances, but nothing like the moment on the balcony or the way time froze when I touched her.

Although I found more entertainment in talking to her than I probably should have, each moment that I put my energy into benefiting Hutchington Enterprises, I withered. I didn't want to help this rich man find new ways to hurt society and the planet for his gain. Was I any better than him with my complacency?

Was I any better than the sellout my dad always said I would be?

Well, with any luck, I wouldn't be working with Hutchington long.

"Everyone is going to talk social media strategy, but clearly he doesn't want to hear that until the face-to-face." I fidgeted with the stem of my wine glass, watching the bubbles cling to the edge.

"Why is that clear?"

I was vaguely aware of her reaching for her water. "Because—" I stuttered on my thought when she moved past her sweating glass. "Because, if that's what he wanted"—her finger drew along the base where it rested against the tabletop, and I swallowed—"he'd have arranged appointments, not invitations."

Her knuckle brushed the meat of my thumb, and my hair stood on end.

"That's a good point." She did it again. A shiver ran down my spine.

"We need to charm him." I ran my thumb along the side of her finger.

"Well," she said, pulling her hand back to grab her water and lift it to her lips, "you're the perfect person for that."

A crease pressed between my eyebrows. "Is that a bad thing?"

She lowered her water and spoke to the vicinity of my shoulder. "It'd be easier if you were resistible." She stood. "I'll set the dirty dishes in the hallway. Are you done?"

I nodded. Pleasure warred with pain in my gut. Her wanting me made me feel about ten feet tall, but knowing the toll it caused her did not sit well. Keeping our distance wasn't an option in this hotel room, and it was going to wear on both of us. We needed a new way to get through the next couple of days.

I knew how I'd like to release the pressure between us, but I wouldn't suggest it yet. Not when I didn't know what it would mean to her.

I stepped out of the bathroom. On the bed, Serena sat cross-legged, staring down at Hutchington's metrics. Her skin shone from her face cream, her hair still braided down to the middle of her back. I'd never seen it down before—it was always in a braid or a smooth twist at work. I wanted to take the elastic out of the bottom and shake her dark waves free. Run the strands through my fingers.

She wore green shorts that looked soft to the touch. But her long smooth legs were what I really noticed.

I had just come in the shower, biting down on the knuckle of my free hand to silence myself while I thought of her. The release didn't change the fact that sharing a bed would be absolute torture. And that a few shared moments and a couple of flirtatious smiles over dinner didn't change the fact that she was off-limits.

I strode across the carpet in a pair of gray sweats and an undershirt. Most nights I slept naked and thinking I'd have my own room, I hadn't packed pajamas. Her eyes followed me, and her lips parted. Like I was something she wanted to take a bite out of. She could make an entire meal of me if she wanted.

Standing at my side of the bed, I planted my feet and crossed my arms over my chest, and decided to test something out. I let her take a good look, and I tilted my head when her eyes met mine. Her pupils dilated, black dots surrounded by the richest green.

Maybe it was just flirtation, or maybe it could be something more, at least for a couple of nights. Maybe if we finally stepped over this line, I could begin to think of something other than Serena.

"I'm going to take these sweats off, and unless you wanna see what I've got underneath, you're gonna want to look away, Tulip," I warned.

She licked her lips, and I hoped she'd stay just where she was. Everywhere her gaze landed on me tingled, bright flares on my shoulders and arms, my thighs and hips.

Disappointment bore into my chest as she scooted toward the headboard. Lifting the blankets and sheets, she slid her legs under them, and rolled onto her side, giving me her back. "You do have underwear on, right?"

I snorted. "No, I sleep dick out or not at all. Of course I'm wearing underwear."

Her laughter shook the bed as I slipped under the covers next to her.

My head sank into the pillow, and I looked at the ceiling. "It's safe, you can look now."

She twisted to her other side, the bedding pulling with her movements. "Are *you* a cuddler? I never asked."

"I am." I shifted to my side, facing her. We were separated by mere inches. "If you wanna cuddle, you don't have to fight it on my account."

One corner of her lips quirked up. "You may be trouble, Daire."

I lifted an eyebrow. "You don't have to fight anything on my account," I said softly.

The quiet sound she made in the back of her throat would have been impossible for me to hear if the room wasn't so quiet and if we weren't lying so close.

"Definitely trouble," she whispered.

"I'm no trouble at all. The trouble is the burden and expectations on us." In the dark of the room, all I could see were the whites of her eyes. "Serena, if we don't bend, we'll break."

She sighed. "Maybe, but I don't break easily." She laid on her back. "Good night, Daire."

"Good night."

I closed my eyes, listening to the waves on the shore and her deepening breaths.

Absolutely delicious torture.

Chapter Six

♥

Daire

I woke up to Serena pressed to my back, her breasts soft and full through the fabric of her tank top, her smooth leg draped over my hip, my hand resting on her thigh. The ends of her braid tickled the skin of my bicep, and my nose was filled with that herbal, floral scent. She moaned in the back of her throat, and my erection twitched, bringing me firmly awake. She shifted her hips, the heat of her cunt against my ass. Her second moan sent shivers that made my scalp tingle.

Measures had to be taken immediately.

Gently removing myself from the warmth of her body, I sat on the edge of the bed and snatched my sweats from the floor. Trying not to shift the bed, I put my legs into them and stood, pulling them up and shoving my hard cock unceremoniously into my pants. Judging by Serena's breathing, she was still asleep. Stretching my arms over my head, my stiff muscles resisted warming to the thought of the day, every cell in my body wanting to crawl back under the covers to discover more of her sounds.

Outside the glass door, the sky was still dark.

I looked over my shoulder to find Serena blinking slowly awake.

"Good morning." My voice was raspy from sleep.

She bit her lip and glanced down at the pillow I had just been laying on. "Mmm-hmm."

Looking at her squeezed my heart, and heat poured molten hot into my blood. I needed more distance, or I needed no distance at all—there was no in between. And since she hadn't agreed with me last night when I insinuated that we could give in to temptation, I needed to take care of my cock straining against my pants. I couldn't even whisper an *excuse me*, or it might have come out as something like, *Excuse me, can I stick my face between your legs until your thighs twitch?* Instead, I went to the bathroom without speaking another word.

It didn't take long for me to silently take matters into my own hands—swallowing back my moans as every muscle in my body flexed. When I stepped back into the bedroom, she was where I'd left her. The image my imagination conjured was nothing compared to the actual sight of her. She was beautiful.

She pinched her lower lip in her teeth as her eyes roamed my body, and I nearly turned around and closed the door between us. She was making me feral.

"Can you go get coffee?" she asked.

I forced myself to lean against the door jam and shove my hands in my pockets. "Anything for you, Tulip."

One corner of her lips quirked up. "So, 'Tulip' is officially a thing, huh?"

"Does it offend you?"

"Would you stop if it did?"

"Of course."

She smiled. "Coffee with cream. Lots of cream."

"Are you always so demandin'?" My voice was light, but I was sure my eyes were anything but.

My mouth went dry when she licked her lips and nodded. "I like to get exactly what I want."

My focus narrowed to only her mouth, my thoughts were filth and fire. I shook my head to clear it. "What exactly do you want from me?"

"Just a little bit of playful flirting. That's all it can really be. Okay?" she asked, her voice breathy.

"Okay." It felt like gasoline tossed on an already blazing fire, but if it was what she wanted, I could give her that.

I stood straight. She sat up, propping herself with her hands on either side of her hips. I lifted an eyebrow and shook my head when she pressed her biceps against her breasts. The thin fabric of her tank top did nothing to conceal the peaked tips of her nipples.

The breath gushed out of me from between pursed lips. "I'm a very fun toy, Serena, but retaliation is fair play. Remember that," I warned.

"I can take it."

Before I could draw any more insinuations from those four little words, I turned for the door. "I'll be back in a few."

"Extra cream, please."

"I remember. I'll give you exactly what you want."

When I return with a coffee in each hand, she had put a sweatshirt on, but she was still wearing those little green shorts. And I could still feel the texture of the skin of her thigh under my palm, draped across my hip.

"Hi." She looked up from the binder in her lap, another open next to her on the bed.

I set her cup on her bedside table and nodded toward a graph showing tweets referencing Hutchington. There was an uptick in his mentions recently, most of them negative. Quite a few of them were from an environmental non-profit called Planted Future, but they were by no means the only group.

A different group's name stood out on the page. Sustainably Green was known for its finesse within the public eye, and they used that finesse to assist large corporations in cutting their emissions and adopting a more environmentally friendly way of doing business. They'd reached out to Hutchington many times in the past few years, but he'd been outspoken in his dismissal of their agenda.

Not for the first time, I questioned my conflict of interests. "See anything new?" I asked.

"No, but I don't like to be surprised."

I nodded. If she ever decided to leave Garcia Public Relations, there would be a long line of firms anxious to bring her on. Just working with her for the last few months, I'd learned more than I had at any of my other employers. When I'd taken this position, I hadn't expected it to be long-term, but even so, my plans had accelerated unexpectedly recently.

I considered my side of the bed and decided it was probably best that I didn't fill it. Instead, I pulled a chair across the floor and sat. I propped my ankle on my knee and took a sip of my drink.

She wrapped her hand around the paper sleeve on her cup. I'd never envied a plastic lid before, but then she pressed it to her lips. "Thank you for the coffee."

"Is it enough cream?"

"It is."

"I told you I was good."

She smirked. "I never had any doubt." After setting her drink down, she handed me a binder. "See if you see anything."

I grunted in affirmation and took the material. I set it propped in the triangle of my leg. It did not make for ergonomic positioning.

The most exciting moment of the morning was when Serena took a drink from my cup and not hers. "Oh my god, what is that?"

I threw my head back on my stiff neck and laughed. "Tea."

"You would pick *this* over coffee?"

"Yes."

"That's..." She shook her head. "You are not to be trusted."

Oh, Tulip, if you only knew.

We ordered salads from room service for lunch and ate with our faces pressed to our tablets displaying even more metrics.

When it felt like I hadn't blinked in a week and I couldn't identify one number from another on the screen, I announced, "I either need to sleep or go for a walk."

She raised an eyebrow. "Don't have the stamina?"

I pushed my plate to the side and crossed my arms on the tabletop. "Why would you do this to me?" I groaned.

With a coquettish flutter of her eyes, she shrugged. "It's okay, it's completely natural, nothing to be embarrassed about. Take a nap. We'll try again later."

Hiding my smile behind my fist, I considered her. The mischievous tilt of her lips. The playful gleam in her green eyes. The challenging tilt of her chin.

I stood. "You're right. Nothin' to be ashamed of."

Her shoulders sank, her defenses dropping the smallest increment.

I stretched my arms over my head, well aware that an inch or so of my abs would show. "You're welcome to join me."

The rise and fall of her chest halted, caught between her parted lips. I turned my back to her to stop myself from brushing my thumb along her mouth. I didn't have to look to know she was watching me as I hooked my thumbs into the waistline of my sweats and pushed them down.

She didn't make a sound the whole time. I couldn't even hear her exhale.

I crawled under the covers and looked at her over my shoulder. "You should get some rest too, Tulip."

"Deviant."

"Wouldn't you like to know?"

The groan at the back of her throat nearly threw me over a ledge.

I closed my eyes and took deep breaths willing my body to calm, well aware that I wouldn't be able to sleep.

Chapter Seven

♥

Serena

I sat on the balcony, wondering if I should wake Daire up. We needed to start getting ready for the party soon. But after watching him slide his pants down his boxer-clad ass, revealing his strong thighs, I didn't fully trust myself to be near him in bed. Not when this morning, I'd almost given in to the struggle of resisting him.

Before I even opened my eyes, my body ached for Daire. I was vaguely aware of the weight of his hand on my thigh, then his shifting out of bed woke me fully. Every time I'd roused in the night, I found myself crowding his side, the warmth of his skin feeding into mine. Unlike every other time, I didn't roll back to where I belonged. There was no use trying to fall back asleep now, not when my hands had learned the curve of his solid bicep. Not when my shin now knew the scrape of the hair on his calf.

My body was a sea of want, needing him to dive in.

He stood with his back to me and stretched. He groaned with his hands fisted above his head and his elbows bent. His biceps stretched the short sleeves of his white shirt, the thin fabric clinging to the lines of his back and shoulders. I could practically feel the strong planes under my hands. The cotton of his boxer briefs clung to the curves of his ass and the corded muscles of his thighs.

When he disappeared into the bathroom, I took the chance to press my face into his pillow and breathe in the scent he left behind. It was clean and almost sweet. I gripped the sheets—still warm from him.

All traces of the lust-crazed pillow-sniffer were gone when he emerged from the bathroom, wearing the jeans he'd worn the evening before. They sat low on his hips and clung to his thighs.

I loved them. I really wanted to take them off.

My phone buzzed with a text from Willow, making me aware that I was staring into space lost in thought and lust.

Any news? Has he admitted to stealing thousands of dollars from us?

I rolled my eyes. *No.*

Lexi texted next, *We have no evidence it's him.*

You are all over the place on this, Lex, Willow pointed out. *Just yesterday you were talking about how this one-room thing could be an opportunity.*

She could just as easily prove his innocence.

How is the one-room thing going, btw? Miya asked.

I bit my lip, wondering how much to say. Willow knew about my crush on Daire, and even though Miya and Lexi were my really good friends, I hadn't told them how I felt about him.

I was so engrossed in thinking up a response that Daire's sudden "Hey" made me gasp and press my phone to my chest.

The sliding door opening must have been lost in the sound of the wind and the ocean.

He shoved his hands in his pockets. "Sorry, I didn't mean to sneak up on you."

"No, it's okay, I'm a pretty jumpy person."

"Should we start getting ready?"

I nodded.

My phone continued to buzz with texts in my hand as I reached my arms toward the blue sky and arched my back. I didn't think much about how my sweatshirt silhouetted my body—it was old, comfy, and loose-fitting—but his eyes darkened with a heat I'd seen before but still wasn't accustomed to. It quickened an ache in my core.

He was the ultimate temptation, and my resistance was growing thin. That must have been why I couldn't stop dancing with the trouble we would make. "I really like that."

His voice sounded as if it had been scraped through sandpaper. "What?"

"When you look at me... like that."

His chest rose with a deep breath.

I stood. "I'll get dressed first."

The balcony was small, and just standing put me inches away from him. I shuffled sideways between him and the empty chair. The binder was pressed to my chest, like a shield between him and me. But it didn't keep my bare thighs from brushing his jean-covered legs. Without me telling it to, my body stopped moving. It lingered.

I gave in, just a little bit. Just enough. Dear Lord, let it be enough.

Leaning into him, I pressed my forehead to the crook of his shoulder.

We both sighed. The smallest contact fed a starving part of me. He gripped the sides of my sweatshirt, bunching it in his fists, pulling me just a little tighter. He rested his chin atop my head. Inside I cried out for more, and it took all of my willpower to pull away. Willpower that I knew wouldn't hold out much longer.

His grip eased, giving me more room.

I didn't look up into his eyes as I built space back between us. I knew what I'd see there. Longing. Desire. Intimacy.

I'd convinced myself that we could flirt and nothing would come of it, but judging by the shiver down my spine at just the merest contact, I was lying to myself.

This game we were playing was getting dangerous. If we kept pulling each other's strings, eventually one of us would unravel.

I had a sneaking suspicion that it would be me. That I was the only hold out between us.

And when I broke it would be entirely. There wouldn't be any semblance of dipping my toe in the water. No, I would dive headfirst without much thought to how deep the waters were or how hurt I could get on impact.

I couldn't find my underwear. I knew I'd grabbed them out of my suitcase when I'd draped my dress over my arm before going into the bathroom to change. But they were nowhere in sight. Gripping the hanger of my dress, I shook it, but they did not fall out.

I might have forgotten to grab them. I had been a bit distracted today.

Okay, very distracted, and horny as fuck. All. Fucking. Day. Today felt like a fever dream. Each of us taking a step a little bit closer to danger. Our words perfectly innocent, but laced with suggestion.

It was wildly inappropriate of me. He was my subordinate. Only minutes ago, Lexi texted that they found another false consulting account—still within the months Daire had been working with us. My behavior was deplorable... but I could not stop. And worse, I didn't want to.

I was a match just needing a strike to set me aflame.

I needed to focus on the party tonight.

In only my strapless bra, I stepped into my dress, shuffling my hips to get the gown's waist over them. The scrape of the fabric left a memory on my skin—the ghost of a touch.

Sliding the zipper to the top was a bit of a struggle with my hair undone at my back. In the mirror, I double-checked the fit. I had a backup dress if this didn't feel right. But the sheath style with the pencil skirt emphasized a "classic Americana" silhouette.

I did still need underwear, though.

Daire was lounging against the hotel table when I opened the door. His auburn eyebrows lifted at the sight of me. Even though he took an eyeful of me and I knew it was a terrible idea for me to indulge in the sight of him, I didn't stop myself.

That was my problem with him... I couldn't fucking stop myself.

His reddish-gold scruff caught the light streaming in through the sliding glass door. His white T-shirt strained on his biceps, his arms crossed over his chest. There was a fine dusting of freckles on his knuckles and forearms. Were they on his stomach? Were they everywhere? Taking a leisurely path down the line of his legs, my gaze landed near his bare feet crossed at the ankle, a pale speckling of freckles on the top of his foot.

Right next to his foot was the smallest scrap of black lace.

My eyes widened.

He smirked as he bent into my line of vision. Hooking the crotch of my panties on one finger, he straightened, then looked up at me through long lashes.

My core clenched.

"Did you forget somethin'?" he asked.

I would never consider myself shy, but there was a thimble-sized amount of embarrassment swirling with arousal. My initial instinct was to snatch the underwear from him, toss a "Thank you" over my shoulder, and disappear into the bathroom. But he'd positioned himself here to toy with me. Waiting for who-knows-how-long while I got dressed.

It was within the boundaries of our little game. But the boundaries were growing tight. Couple that with my inherent competitive nature... I could play just a little longer.

The carpet was coarse on the pads of my feet as I walked toward him. Licking my lower lip, I took the black lace off of the curve of his finger.

"I did." My voice was nearly a purr.

He looked down his straight sharp nose as I looked up at him. We were close, possibly a foot and a half apart. I spread my fingers inside the leg holes, the waistband stretched across the backs of my hands.

I turned my side to him, flipping my hair over the shoulder opposite him. Bending, I pointed my toe to thread my foot into the thong.

"What are ye doin'?"

I paused balanced on one foot. "Well, I can't go without any underwear on."

The grin slipped from his face. His palm scraped across his jaw.

I lifted a questioning eyebrow. "If you'd be more comfortable, you can go in the bathroom."

A muscle flexed in his jaw. "Would ye like me to go?"

"You do whatever you want."

His copper eyes met mine. "I'll stay right here then."

My movements were slow and controlled as my heart raced, thrumming an anxious rhythm. I slid my other foot into place. The lace scraped a soft trail up my calves.

He watched me with such hot intensity. It was *torture*. I forced myself to languish with each inch despite the riotous desire my insides had become. My lungs demanded more air. But I only allowed myself slow, even breaths.

I was the appearance of composure.

The illusion almost faltered when he let out a guttural sigh as I hiked up my skirt, showing him the lower curve of my ass. I smoothed the lace around my hips with the slide of my fingers, my knuckles brushing my skin.

I brushed my skirt back in place. Twisting, I checked for wrinkling over my ass and then peeked over at Daire.

His hands were buried in his copper hair—his fingers dug trails along his scalp. Defined strong muscles flexed on either side of his head. His jaw was clenched. His chest rose and fell in deep measured breaths.

He was a man barely restrained.

My voice came out hesitant and breathy. "Get dressed."

He looked at me for a few more moments, his eyes lit like flames, raging and almost wild.

I silently begged him to cross that line. The one that we'd been toeing for months, the one I could barely maintain here, alone with him. The one that would finally put me out of my misery.

Every word, every almost touch, every moment of intimacy was tearing down my barriers. And I didn't want them anymore. I'd built them to protect me, but now they only caused me pain.

I wanted Daire.

But he nodded, grabbed his suit from the closet, and disappeared into the bathroom.

I was surprised to realize when I blinked that my eyes stung. It didn't make any sense, but none of my behavior made sense. My priorities were mangled and twisted, and there wouldn't be any relief until I finally gave in to desire.

Chapter Eight

♥

Daire

The drive from the resort to Hutchington's mansion was similar to the one from the airport—winding highway and my constant struggle to watch the road and not Serena. The top was up on the convertible this time. Serena's perfume was subtle, but it flooded my senses in the closed space. The urge to bury my face in the curve of her neck to breathe her in was almost overwhelming.

All of my urges were overwhelming.

Over the past twenty-four hours, I'd grown saturated in want. She was under my skin. She was behind my eyelids when I blinked. She was in my lungs and coursing through my veins.

The world had shrunk to only the two of us. The winding neighborhood streets lined with gated driveways were just a backdrop. We were what was real.

Her skin kissed by the sun was real. The bright vivid image burned into my brain of her fingers reaching up her skirt was real. Her power over me was real. She could keep me on my toes. I'd always been able to anticipate other people's behaviors, but I was growing to understand that whatever she did next, I wouldn't see it coming.

There was a thrill in the not knowing.

I followed a black car into the driveway, one of many being parked by valets.

I tossed the keys in the jogging valet's hand, and then I followed Serena into the grand foyer of the house. Keeping my eyes at her shoulder or higher was a struggle. Especially when I remembered the curve of her ass, her fingers beneath her skirt.

My head was not at work. My head was dreaming up all of the ways I wanted to wrap her around me.

My thoughts must have been etched onto my face because when she looked at me, her eyebrows shot up and her pupils dilated.

"I'm going to..." she trailed off.

I nodded. "Yeah, me too." We went in opposite directions.

Interminable hours later, the party was in full swing. Serena mingled with a group of our competitors a couple of feet away. Almost by accident, I found myself in a gathering with Hutchington, an eccentric, elderly man. His hands gestured wildly, and he told stories as if he'd never had to prove himself interesting. The money he spent on the party could have made a significant difference in environmental conservation if he cared to actually *do* good instead of paying people like me to simulate the *appearance* of good.

I was annoyed, and he functioned only as a distraction from the person I really wanted to watch and listen to. She was so close. No matter how many times I tried to force my mind and eyes away from her, they always found her.

I couldn't stop staring at her. The black dress highlighted the curves of her body. Her mouth pressed against the rim of a champagne flute. Her hair pulled into a smooth twist at the back of her head. I didn't understand how she could contain all of that length in a twist. Back in our room, it had fallen on her shoulders in flowing layers—wild and beautiful as she toyed with me.

I forced my attention on the chatter around me, interjecting my thoughts whenever appropriate if only to keep my mind on the conversation. My plans didn't rely on this meeting. In fact, I never planned to work with Hutchington. But this was what Serena wanted, and that was enough for me to refocus my efforts.

And then she glanced my way, a ghost of a smile on her lips, and my efforts wavered.

With a little lift of her glass, she shifted to join the circle opposite me. My eyes raked up the length of her legs, to her waist, to her full breasts. My appraisal may have been brief, but the moment our gazes locked, it was clear she'd noticed. It was difficult to keep a polite expression.

With her near, I did not feel polite.

As soon as I had an opportune moment, I exited the conversation.

Running my hand down my face, I loosened my clenched jaw and pinched my tie between two fingers to shift the knot a little looser—not enough to look disheveled, but enough that maybe I could breathe.

At the bar, I ordered a glass of whiskey. My back was to her, but I could practically feel her pull tugging at me. I nodded a thanks to the bartender and found another group to pretend to be interested in.

Discreetly, I watched her over the brim of my glass. The observant way she listened. The confidence as she spoke. Whatever she'd said was clearly the right thing to say because Hutchington smiled and nodded. She gave me a smug look over her shoulder. Her eyes landed on me without scanning the room—she knew exactly where I was.

It was our job to interact with the rest of the attendees, not each other, but I wanted nothing more than to have all of her to myself. To discover all of her hidden twists and turns. She was playful and risky, yet effortlessly in control. I wanted to know how she unraveled. How could I undo her? Undress her?

Fuuuck.

"My beautiful guests, if you would join me in the media room," our host bellowed.

The party moved towards the in-home theater. Just an hour or so longer, and we could return to our hotel room, and I could see what Serena's flirtation really meant. We had at least one more night. We could make the most of it. We might be able to douse these flames before going back to Chicago where she was firmly out of my reach.

But then, if everything went according to plan, and if she didn't end up hating me, maybe we could actually go on that date we'd canceled months ago.

She lingered at the back, and I waited for a few people to pass to join her. If we were brief, she could tell me what I missed in her conversation with Hutchington and we could adjust our plan if necessary. As everyone else turned into the theater, I pulled her into an empty room. It had a large wooden desk and bookshelves lined with leather-bound tomes, clearly more for looks than for actual reading. I turned the lock on the handle. We only had a few minutes, and I didn't want to be interrupted.

When I turned around, she was slipping her thong down her thighs, her skirt pushed up just below her cunt.

"Fuck me," I hissed.

Regardless of my brain screaming what a terrible idea this was, my cock did not agree.

She froze, her eyes wide with horror. "Is this not what we're here for?"

I closed the distance between us in two strides.

"It is fuckin' now," I growled in a voice strange to my ears.

Bending my knees, I slid my hands under her hips and finally took hold of her. My fingers sank into the flesh of her ass and squeezed. But the fulfilled fantasy was short-lived, only for the fact that I had other more pressing needs. I should have been gentler as I set her on the edge of the desk, but I wasn't in a gentle state of mind.

I wasn't in *any* state of mind. I might as well have been a howling dog in an old cartoon.

The fabric of my suit scraped against my erection as I dropped to my knees on the carpet. I tore the lace from around her knees. "Get your skirt outta my fuckin' way."

With my face inches from her cunt, I could smell her arousal. She shifted on her hips and pulled her dress up higher. I followed with my mouth, biting and kissing up her inner thighs, her legs widening to give me more room. And then my tongue found her wet and salty-sweet.

So fuckin' sweet.

She gasped and arched her back as I spread her lips wider with my thumbs.

My erection throbbed a persistent plea to slip into her heat.

I wanted to bend her over the desk and sink inside of her. To find out all of the different ways to make her squeeze around me, but that'd have to come later. My only need at this moment was to make her come as quickly and quietly as possible.

Her hips rocked, her clit against my face. The only sounds were her quick sharp breaths and our skin scraping together. My cheeks and jaw and nose were slick with her wetness. I wanted to keep tasting her, let her orgasm mount, but there wasn't time for that.

I was so fuckin' hard for this woman.

The buckle of my belt jingled as I slipped it open, and I pulled my face away for the barest of seconds.

"No," she whined.

Her head fell back as I sank two fingers into her.

"So fuckin' wet," I groaned, swiping the palm of my hand down her slit. With my glistening hand, I gripped my aching cock. Her eyes were hungry as she watched me stroke myself before filling her with the fingers of my other hand.

"Yes." Her whisper was more of a breath escaping from lips that I hadn't even gotten to taste yet. She laid down fully on the solid desktop, the heels of her shoes sharp on my jacketed back, urging me closer.

I flicked my tongue on her clit, and her walls tightened around my fingers. If she could squeeze my fingers like this... My hold firmed around my shaft, my release growing closer.

Hers was too. I could feel it coiling ever tighter. I could hear it in her held breath.

I licked and gently sucked while stroking her deep inside.

She spasmed in waves. Her dress bunched at her waist robbed me of seeing her.

I stood. She heaved deep breaths, her tits full and heavy against the neckline of her dress. My cock jumped at each of her shivers of pleasure. I needed to come. Stroking, I held her ruined thong at my tip.

But then she knelt before me, and I was suddenly, blissfully at the back of her throat. I sucked in a breath between clenched teeth. I didn't realize I was holding the back of her head until I felt the pins hidden in her hair stab into my palm as I thrust into her hungry mouth. Except for my breathing and her soft choking sounds, we were silent.

I had to grab the edge of the desk for support as I came—my mouth opened in a silent moan.

She swallowed me down.

Her eyes glistened, as she looked up at me. My cock slipped from her beautifully swollen red lips. Her makeup was still perfectly intact.

Chapter Nine

♥

Serena

I could not believe what we did.

What I did.

Seriously, what was I thinking? My torn underwear was in the interior pocket of Daire's jacket. Even worse, every time I remembered that fact I got wet all over again. The way his expression changed from shock to desire. The way he dropped me on the edge of the desk. The way he went to work on me like my orgasm was his dream job.

I made the most thoughtless decision of my life, and I couldn't even regret it. Daire was trouble, and I needed to go back to the time when we didn't speak. When coming against his striking face was fantasy only.

Back when my worst behavior was inappropriate flirting, not face-fucking at a dinner party for work.

The most reckless decision of my adult life hadn't taken very long—I'd come in a million little pieces in record time.

He must have been thinking the same thing because we hadn't spoken since we left the study, and rejoined the party as if nothing was amiss. No one even seemed to notice that we were missing when we stepped into the theater room. We were presentable. I was even able to fix my hair with a little help, his fingers gently pinning the strands into place.

Mr. Hutchington promised us he'd be in touch, and I was too shocked with myself to feel anything.

Pulling up to the hotel, Daire slid into a parking spot.

We walked into the lobby, in silence.

We rode the elevator, in silence.

We strode down the hallway, in silence.

He slid the key out of his pocket—the same pocket that held my *underwear.*

What was I thinking?

I was thinking I couldn't forget the groan he'd made as I let him see the barest hint of my ass. The goddamn way his biceps flexed when I'd straightened my dress down my legs. The way his copper eyes looked at me like a panther did its prey.

I was thinking I'd been wet for him for months and I wanted to be filled.

I was thinking that I couldn't fight any longer.

Sitting on the edge of the bed, I slipped my shoes off.

"Serena?"

Had I ever heard him say my name before? It was a new language inside his mouth, the "r" rolled from the back of his throat. It was delightfully filthy, and I could not for the life of me explain why.

I managed a "Hmm?"

"Are you ashamed?"

His words cut through all of my bullshit to strike my heart. I looked up and met his eyes. He must have seen the truth there because he asked, "Why?"

"Daire," I admonished, "we just—"

"I know what we did." He licked his lips. "I can still fuckin' taste you."

I squirmed.

It only encouraged him. "We lost our heads—"

I scoffed.

"—but denying this, us, is only gonna make it happen again," he continued.

My core clenched, and my entire body wanted nothing more than for it to happen again.

"But we can be smarter about where it happens next time." He hooked a finger under my chin. "What do you think?"

My brain was mush. What were thoughts? I stared up at him, his thumb rested on the fullest part of my lip.

"Tulip?"

Through my eyelashes, I looked up into his copper eyes. His head tilted. He was cast from marble, held perfectly still—waiting for my next word.

"I don't know." I couldn't formulate a plan when I was trapped in our immediate past and my emotions were a confusing combination of desire and shame.

His finger fell from my chin.

"Come back," I whispered. Desperation surged above all other feelings at the loss of his touch.

He sat on the bed next to me. The sleeve of his suit brushed my arm, but otherwise, we didn't touch.

I rested my head on his shoulder. "I can't believe we did that."

When he'd pulled me into that study and locked the door, any other purpose than to finally find release hadn't even crossed my mind. He was right—not having him felt like denying myself something vital. When I finally gave in, my lungs filled with new air. I could see new colors. I wanted more of what the world looked like with Daire in it.

"I'm rather shocked as well." He reached for the knot of his tie and loosened it. "It was not a great idea."

"No, it wasn't."

"But I would do it again."

Turning my head, I met his unwavering gaze. I recognized passion there, but there was something else I hadn't seen from him before. It took me a moment to place tenderness and vulnerability.

I licked my lips. "Me too."

He shifted his face inches from mine. "That happened because we got to a boil. There is something between us that we can't ignore."

It took the barest of movements for me to press my forehead to his. "I don't want to ignore it."

"We have one more night."

"It won't be enough."

"No. It won't." His mouth brushed the corner of mine. "But do you think that would have happened there if I'd been givin' it to you good, the way you need it? If last night and this morning, instead of givin' myself a yank thinking of your sweet cunt, I slipped into you good and proper?"

A groan vibrated at the back of my throat. My hips rolled at the pressure building between my thighs.

His hand hovered where my skirt ended and my skin began. The warmth of his skin seeped into me, but he didn't actually touch me. "Do you think that would have happened, if I stretched your tight cunt around my cock? If we'd put an end to all of this teasing, and we used every inch of this giant fuckin' bed?"

The pad of his thumb swiped back and forth along the hem of my dress.

"What do you think, Tulip?"

Even the logical side of my brain screamed that he had a solid argument.

I would not have believed that I could speak in full sentences if the words hadn't come out of my mouth. "I don't know what would have happened." Reaching between us, I gripped the knot of his tie in one hand and pulled it loose with the other, unraveling it just like my resistance. Nuzzling my nose just under his ear, I placed a kiss on the thin skin at his racing pulse.

"Fuck." His fingers slipped under my skirt and dug into the flesh of my thigh.

His heart drummed into my palm as I pressed my hands to his chest and rotated to straddle him. The fabric of his slacks scraped my wet, tender cunt, and I groaned. The cool air of the room hit my ass as he pushed my skirt to my waist. His hands roamed the expanse of my ass, pressing my flesh up. The tips of his fingers sank in.

I sat back onto his lap and slowly pulled the pins out of my twisted hair. Then his hands joined mine, gentle tugs that sent sparklers under my skin. When the strands were loose and wild down my back, he cupped my skull, his fingers curling and releasing, a gentle tug that promised more.

I arched my back, pressing against the chest of his re-spectable gray suit and his crisp white shirt. I reached between us and undid the top two buttons before his teeth gently sank into the flesh of my earlobe.

With the air rushing out of my lungs, I whispered, "Stretch me out."

Our mouths finally met, desperate and demanding. My taste was there on his lips, his tongue gliding against mine. It re-minded me of the heat of our first time, the sharp orgasm that ripped through me. Then the salty taste of his come as he thrust into my mouth. Followed by only our ragged breaths, desperate for each other and our need to not get caught.

He brought out the side of me that was reckless and wanton.

One of his hands fisted in my hair, and the other wrapped around my back. I clung to his shoulders. The solid expanse only fueled my desire to touch and grope the rest of him. To see where his freckles thickened and faded. To have the full force of his lithe, powerful body spear deep inside of me.

I wrapped my leg around his waist as he rotated me under-neath him on the bed. We crawled to the center, our mouths still searching for more to taste and suck and bite—a single form of legs and hands and lust.

"On your stomach," he ordered.

At the same moment, I said, "Take off your clothes."

We both groaned, knowing that meeting either command would mean regrettable space between our bodies. But he managed to pull away and stood to tug his arms out of his suit coat, then yank the tails of his shirt free to throw it over his head. Every layer removed displayed more of him that I wanted to see and touch.

Why did humans wear so many clothes?

It was a sin to keep anything so beautiful concealed.

I was too busy watching his undressing to remember that I had my own layers to undo. I sat up and reached for the zip at the base of my neck and pulled it down. His hands halted at his belt as I slipped the arms of my dress down. My breasts pushed out of the top of my strapless bra, barely covering my nipples. The black fabric of the dress bunched around my waist, and I laid back to press my feet to the mattress and lift my hips to shimmy it off.

He sat there frozen with a white-knuckled grip on his belt, while his eyes caressed every inch of my newly bared skin. When I couldn't take anymore, I sat up and reached for him. The jingle of metal, then the hiss of leather filled the space between us. I unbuttoned his slacks and lowered his zipper as he ran a finger along the curves of my breasts. My nipples pinched, begging for more of his touch.

"You're so fuckin' gorgeous."

I'd never been short on confidence, but the reverence in his voice made me feel worshiped. The ends of my hair tickled across my shoulders as he brushed it off of my back, then there was a tightening and then the release of the clasps at my back coming undone.

My bra fell to my lap, and he stepped just out of my reach. His pants opened, and the outline of his erection was visible against the black cotton of his boxer briefs. Gripping the hem of his undershirt, he pulled it over his head.

"Oh my god," I groaned at the sight of his lean, ridged torso.

I could hear the smirk in his voice, but I was too busy indulging in the dusting of reddish-brown hair on his chest to meet his gaze. "Lie back. I want to see you too."

I didn't pay any attention to where my bra landed as I tossed it aside. Instead, I laid back as he had commanded, my tits bouncing and settling into my armpits as I did, and he groaned in appreciation. Fueled by his brazen appreciation, I ran my hand down my stomach and over the dark curls of my mound. He watched my fingers slip between my slit for the barest of seconds before he groaned again and pushed his pants and boxers down. In the same motion, he climbed on top of me. I didn't get to look at him the way I wanted to, but his mouth was hot and wet on my nipples, licking and sucking. All I could do was writhe and gasp, arching my back and pressing more firmly into his mouth and palm.

His erection grazed against my upper thigh, too far away from my throbbing clit and wet entrance.

He worked sounds of pleasure from me that I had never heard before. His auburn hair was thick and curled around my fingers. I didn't know if I was urging him to stay there or pull back so I could get what I really needed.

"Where are you going?" I gasped when he abruptly stood again.

"Condom" was his only uttered response.

"Hurry." I pressed my knees together and slid my hands over my breasts, too horny to wait for his touch to return.

"Fuck me," he groaned.

"Get back over here and I will." My frustration was obvious in my voice. His naked body only made it worse. The dark freckles on his pale skin ended in a V down his stomach and a trail of auburn hair burned bright around his hard, thick, ruddy cock.

He was going to fill me all the way up.

He gave me a lopsided smile and an arrogant lift of his eyebrow when I finally met his gaze. "You want it, Tulip?"

"Yes."

The muscles in his forearm flexed as he rolled the latex over his erection. He trailed urgent kisses up my legs and body as he crawled over me. His mouth met mine at the same moment that the firm tip of him pressed at my entrance. He sank in slowly, careful to fill me hard inch by hard inch. A moan tore from me when he was finally seated fully inside of me, my walls stretched tight around his shaft. I felt his grin against my mouth as his body rolled and eased back inside of me, hitting a spot that took the pressure mounting inside of me and amplified it.

Again and again.

My nails dug into the flexing muscles of his ass. My begs and pleas for *more* and *just like that* and *don't stop* were interrupted by his tongue plundering my mouth. My breath caught in my chest and my eyes squeezed tight, and my body erupted in a torrent of electricity and the crashing of sensations along every molecule of my body.

He pushed one last time all the way inside of me, groaning with his teeth pressed against my shoulder.

Chapter Ten

Daire

Hours, an email from Hutchington, and a quick trip to a store for more condoms later, Serena was draped across my chest. I trailed my knuckles up and down the curve of her hip to her waist and back, feeling the steady expansion and release of her ribs as she breathed.

The time before our last time, I'd thought that I'd spent all of my energy. But then I'd nestled my nose into Serena's neck where her herbal scent was strongest and I needed her again.

Now, surely, I was completely and totally spent. I was somewhere between unconsciousness and delirium due to incredible orgasms. Then there was Serena, almost surreal in her beauty and passion.

She turned her head to look up at my face. "You're really charming."

I snorted. "Thank you. I'm charmed by you as well."

"No, it's not just me. You're *really* charming. Everyone loves you and wants to be around you."

She pushed against my chest, but I tightened my arms around her shoulders. "No, don't go. Let's sleep like this."

When she strained against my hold, I let her go.

"Why are you so charming?"

"It's kinda my job."

"There are loads of publicists that are not charming at all."

"It's just who I am?" The words were meant to be a statement, but a question mark snuck in at the end.

"That's what I thought originally, but you always know the right thing to say. Like when we got back and I was freaking out... but now I'm here—" She gestured encompassing our naked bodies and the bed. "And it's literally the worst idea ever—"

"Is it?" I scoffed, but she kept speaking as if I hadn't said anything.

"But I have just had the best night of my life. And you talked me right down. How?"

I pushed myself up on my elbows. "Do you feel I manipulated you?"

She shook her head. "Not at all. I'm so about being here. But it's like... How did you do it?"

I licked my lips and contemplated her question. There was an easy answer, one that wouldn't reveal anything. A shrug with an easy *I've just always been this way*. It's the answer I would have given her before, but it wasn't the one I wanted to give her now.

"My da... he's a hard man..." It was an absurd understatement, five words to blanket a childhood full of damage. I drew in a deep breath, and let it out. "It got better when I learned how to control the mood."

Serena held my gaze, her green eyes compassionate.

I let the silence stretch for as long as I could, feeling for the first time truly undressed in front of her.

I quirked my lips. "And I'm Irish. Americans love an Irish accent."

Her smile was quick and knowing.

And I suddenly missed my unexpected moment of vulnerability. "Charm... is an easy shield. People don't really need to know me—they just need to *like* me."

I relaxed back down to the bed when she swung her leg over me to straddle my hips. Cupping my jaw, she ran her thumbs across my cheeks, and the scruff of my unshaven beard rustled into the quiet room.

"I like *knowing* you."

The conviction in her voice tightened a vise around my heart.

The strands of her thick, dark hair tunneled through my fingers as I cradled the back of her head and urged her against me again. Her lips were soft and wet and familiar. I'd kissed her dozens of times since that first kiss only a few hours before, but this time felt achingly like discovering home. It was more than a means to find pleasure and give pleasure.

It was an offering. It was acceptance.

I wanted both.

And it made me uneasy, not knowing what that *want* meant.

Her hips rocked against mine, her slit slick against my erection.

"Serena," I whispered against her mouth.

"Yes?" she whispered back. Her head fell back when I tugged her hair, giving me access to her throat.

What is this? I asked silently, too afraid of the unfurling and coiling of feelings beating from my heart to speak the words aloud. They were too new and quick for me to know where to put them to be safe from them, but too bright for me to ignore. I tried to hide from them in the physical sensations of touching her and the excitement that her gasps and moans sent through me. I cupped her breasts and circled her beaded nipples with my thumbs. She sucked in a quick breath, her ribs expanding and pressing her more firmly into my hands.

I ground my shaft against her clit.

I could feel her groan dance down every single one of my vertebrae.

My face was still hidden against her neck, the dark strands of her hair tangled in my beard and eyelashes.

I was seconds away from rolling her underneath me and onto her stomach, where I could fill her and still conceal whatever it was that threatened my stability, when she stilled, lifting onto her knees slightly. My fingers flexed on her tits to keep from pushing her hips back down, but I forced myself to stop.

"Am I hurting you?" My voice raked against the tight constraint of my throat.

She shook her head. "No, I just want to slow down."

I swallowed and pressed my forehead to the crook of her neck. "I don't know if I can."

With the tender movements of someone dealing with a scared injured animal, Serena trailed her fingers up my forearms, and then my wrists, and then finally to the backs of my hands. She curled her fingers into the spaces between mine and coaxed me to lie back on the bed with our entwined hands. My breathing was faster than normal, and my cock was so hard it hurt, but I stayed still as she stretched to the bedside table where our open box of condoms waited.

She settled atop me and tore the wrapper open. My cock twitched as her fingertips eased the latex down my shaft. She placed my tip at her entrance and took my hands in hers, our palms pressed together.

I clenched my jaw and breathed through my nose.

She squeezed my hands. I looked up from where she hovered above me, wet and slick and hot. "If you need it faster, just tell me."

She lowered, and we both let out a moan. She slowly lifted and lowered over and over again, taking a little more of my length each time. When her ass finally sat on my thighs, I could feel myself at her limit, her cunt tight and flexing around me, trying to pull me deeper even though there was nowhere else to go.

Our hips arched and rocked, and our hands held tight.

But it was her unabashed eye contact that settled my riotous turmoil and soothed my fear.

Our bodies rolled in perfect meter. With each gasping breath and tilt of her back, I watched her orgasm draw near. She bore down on me. I pulled our clasped hands to press a kiss to our knuckles—never taking my eyes off of her.

The sight of her winding tight and then unraveling was the most beautiful thing I'd ever seen. I knew without any doubt that image would be trapped in my memory forever. If I could choose a moment for time to freeze, it would have been that. But then it was gone, and I followed her over the edge.

Distantly, I hoped when I told her my plan, she wouldn't hate me or feel that this moment was wasted on me.

This time, when she draped herself across my chest, we fell asleep, our hands still entwined.

Chapter Eleven

Daire

"What do you mean that was your first time?" Serena demanded. "This weekend?"

A smile spread across my face at her incredulity and... phrasing. "Yes, Tulip, that was my first convertible ride."

I resisted the urge to look at her instead of the coastal roads I was responsible for keeping us on. But I could practically feel her brain splutter like tires spinning on ice. The car's satellite navigation still wouldn't function, so I had her phone in front of me on the dash. Every once in a while, it would buzz with a new text message. I purposefully didn't look down to read them—not only because I was driving, but also because it wasn't any of my business.

She sat back against the passenger seat. "How?"

I shrugged. "I've lived in major cities my whole life. I've never owned a car. Most of my friends don't own cars."

"You're a good driver."

"Yes, I am a competent driver."

"But you've driven before..."

Laughing, I had to look at her, if only to double-check if she wasn't messing with me. She was not.

"Not all cars are convertibles."

"Why haven't you ever rented one, like when you're on vacation?"

"On vacations, I tend to visit family in Ireland. It's not generally ideal weather for having a topless car."

"Huh, I'm disappointed that we can't have it down now. We definitely will on the way back."

We were navigating our way to our one-on-one meeting with Hutchington, and although I loved the way she tilted her face to the sun on our first drive to the resort and the contented upward tilt of her lips as she closed her eyes, we had to be our most presentable.

"Why is it so shocking?" I asked.

"My parents had one when I was a kid. Driving around with the top down was always a lot of fun."

I was struck by the adorable image of a young Serena grinning at the world, hair whipping around her face. I reached over and took her hand, its fit familiar in my grasp even after such a short time. "I'm glad you had that. Where did you grow up?"

"Suburb of Lansing, Michigan."

"What was that like?"

She ran her thumb along the edge of one of my knuckles. "Quaint. Midwestern."

"I picture cows."

Her laugh was throaty and surprised. "There were lots of cows and cornfields and dirt roads."

"Do you ever miss it?"

"No. Sometimes when I go back, every corner feels romantic and nostalgic, but I'm better suited for Chicago. What about you? Do you miss Ireland?"

"Yes, all the time. But at the same time no, I'm also better suited for Chicago."

The intense feelings from the night before were still there, but they were less frightening. Holding her hands and letting our bodies convey what I wasn't ready to say had helped.

There had been so many moments since waking up that I wanted to tell her about my plans. But it didn't seem to be the right time, and really, we were on our way to a potentially career-altering meeting. The more time I spent with her, the more I was convinced that she wouldn't be upset with me. She'd understand.

She seemed to understand everything, to understand me.

We disentangled our fingers before I turned onto the long driveway to Hutchington's mansion. It was unlikely that any-one would notice us holding hands inside the car, but it also wouldn't serve to be caught on any surveillance cam-eras. At the gate, I stated our names and our purpose to the security personnel watching us on their monitor. The large wrought-iron bars swung open.

When we were here before, I had been too tied up in controlling my impulses to really note the gratuitous symbols of wealth. The incredibly manicured lawns and gardens lining the mile-long driveway, the stables off in the distance, the pasture full of horses. The place was huge. *Huge*.

It was always challenging to reconcile this level of osten-tatious wealth with the many issues that could be solved by wealthy people slowing their income growth and/or putting money into social issues that needed it.

I parked the car at the edge of the bricked round-about, where an orange tree grew in the center with a variety of flowers and plants underneath it.

She shot me a smile that landed in my chest, pushing the air from my lungs. "Here we go."

"Here we go."

Opening her door, she climbed out of the car. I took an appreciative look at her ass through the window after she closed the door behind her. I reached for her phone and turned off the navigation app just as a text came through from Willow. I didn't *read* it, but the word *embezzler* practically screamed off of the screen.

You can stop spying on Daire! He's not the embezzler!

I was still trying to make sense of what I'd just read, when another message came through.

Or... at least we have proof that it happened before he showed up... we don't really have proof that he's not involved, but I think it's really unlikely.

Someone was stealing from Garcia Public Relations... and they thought it was me. And Serena was *spying* on me. For the briefest moment, the world tilted.

I locked her phone, turning the screen black. Serena stood just outside my door, her spine straight and shoulders back. Her face was calm with only the slightest bit of questioning in her eyes. I didn't think she'd seen me read her messages, but then I hadn't realized she suspected me of embezzlement.

I thought our connection was authentic... but now, what was it really?

I joined her, while static buzzed in my ears, and I handed her the phone without breaking my stride toward the front door. She met my pace. Vaguely, I understood that she asked me a question, but I couldn't make out the words. I glanced over my shoulder—the sight of her beautiful face stabbing a fresh hole in my heart, and I looked away.

Hutchington greeted us. His white hair was wild, and his blue eyes were stark against his pale skin.

On autopilot, I smiled and shook his hand.

"Daire." His voice broke through my haze. "I wanted to ask last night, what part of Ireland are you from?"

"Dublin. Have you been?" My smile never faltered.

"A few times. I love the city. Lots of history. I'm Irish, actually."

My expression tightened. "Is that right?"

"On my mother's side."

"Lovely." So much smiling, and it already hurt.

We followed him into the home, his assistant quietly trailing behind us.

When he turned into an open door, I was struck by a sickening déjà vu. Without thinking, I glanced at Serena. A polite mask rested on her face.

Hutchington took a seat behind the desk, and I took the chair near the corner where I'd dropped Serena and gone to my knees.

Why had she fucked me? I wanted to believe that the moment we shared in this room was motivated by her need, just as mine was, but there was a disgusting possibility that it had been for a different reason all together. It was possible that every moment I'd grown to cherish had been fabricated. Had there ever even been a booking issue with our room? Or had the shared bed been cultivated to seduce me into divulging secrets?

The worst part was that it had almost worked. My secret was just different than what she thought.

She began our presentation. We had decided on a more conversational approach, as informality seemed to be his preferred approach. I couldn't watch her—it hurt too much. Instead, I struck a confident pose—my ankle crossed over my knee and my back pressed into the seat with an arm draped over the armrest.

The meeting was a blur. We laughed at his jokes. I agreed when necessary. I had planned to be more active, and share the pressure with Serena, but I didn't have anything to give. She didn't seem to need me anyway.

"We'll plan a few opportunities to build the image of Hutchington Enterprise turning a new leaf. A large donation to Planted Futures—"

"Not them," he interrupted.

"I know the blood there is bad, but that's also how we're going to get the most bang for our buck."

He narrowed his eyes, but she didn't squirm under his skepticism.

"What if Hutchington Enterprises really did turn over a new leaf?" I asked.

Just minutes before being the object of Serena's focus had felt like the sun's gentle rays. Now it scorched.

I shifted in my seat. "What if you authentically focused on conservation?"

Hutchington pursed his lips. "Daire, you aren't a tree hugger, are you?"

There was a bitter edge to my voice and smile that I couldn't conceal entirely. "How could I be, when I'm employed by people like you?"

He must not have seen the truth behind my words, because he threw his head back and barked a laugh. "I knew I liked you."

Bile turned in my stomach, but it wasn't at him. It was at myself. It was at becoming exactly what my dad said I would be.

A man whose values could be bought.

Even worse, I was a man who could be duped by a beautiful woman.

My eye caught on something glinting on the carpet near Serena's sensible black heel. I tilted my head to find one of the black pins she'd worn in her hair. The smallest sliver of metal, proof that we were here. That even though it felt like a dream, it had happened. Just like how she made me feel it was safe to open up to her.

It had happened.

It just hadn't been real.

Chapter Twelve

♥

Serena

"Thank you again. This was a wonderful chat." I leaned forward in my chair, fixing Hutchington with my warmest smile.

Daire stared at my foot, and it took him a few moments of silence to stand and extended a hand to Hutchington. "Thank you for having us."

"It was a pleasure. I knew it'd be you two." Hutchington beamed at us from the other side of the desk.

I took his offered hand and shook it. "Does that mean we're in negotiations?"

His eyes crinkled at the corners. "We'll let the lawyers take it from here."

"That's great news. Thank you."

Daire nodded. His smile was beginning to look painful. When he'd seemed off outside, I hadn't thought much of it. When we'd entered this room, it'd taken a moment for me to gather myself, but he hadn't recovered. My body thrummed like an instrument that remembered being played. I'd even had a paranoid moment that it was all a ruse to tell us that Hutchington knew what we did here. On his desk.

Then it was business as usual, and my anxiety settled.

That wasn't the case for Daire. He hadn't been himself at all. Then he'd interrupted our plan to challenge Hutchington.

Luckily, Hutchington seemed to think it was all a joke.

When Daire and I got in the car to leave, I smirked in his direction expecting... something. Instead, his stare was hard out of the windshield, and the tight set of his jaw had replaced the slightly manic smile he'd held for the entirety of our meeting. He turned the key, and the engine sprang to life. He never glanced in my direction.

"What's wrong?" I asked.

He jerked his head as if the sound of my voice hurt him. "I need to focus on driving."

"Are you feeling okay? Do you need me to drive?"

He shook his head and ran a hand down his face.

"Daire, you're making me nervous."

A vein bulged in his throat, his skin bright red from his shirt collar to his hairline. "No need to be, I would just rather have this conversation in our"—he cut himself off and blew out a breath—"the room."

Unease was replaced with outright concern. It crawled under my skin and turned my stomach sour.

"Do you need directions?" I shifted my hips to pull my phone out of my pocket.

"No." His voice was firm, and I settled back into my seat.

I looked out the window. We had been fine on the drive to the meeting. He just hadn't gotten over the shock of the study. But that wasn't right because his behavior had shifted when I'd gotten out of the car. There wasn't anything that I could pinpoint. Beautiful scenery passed us by. Absently, I remembered that we were supposed to have the top down. I'd thought we would have held hands and talked in loud voices over the sound of the wind—then have one last night before we had to face reality and decide what to do next: pretend this never happened, or find a way to change the rules against us dating.

Absently, I opened my phone, and a cold dread sank into my gut. There was an unread text message from Willow: ***But I never really thought it was actually him.***

I opened the conversation and read the previous messages—messages that Daire had probably seen. It was the most logical explanation.

I began formulating a strategy to guide the conversation—one where I was honest, but also where we could land back on good terms and enjoy our last night together.

The twenty-minute drive felt like it stretched on and on, but then Daire pulled into the parking spot that was unofficially ours. We smiled at the clerk behind the desk.

When it was just the two of us in the elevator, I asked, "Can you tell me what's going on?"

"I'd rather wait."

Rushing him wouldn't help my plan. After the conversation yesterday when I was an anxious wreck and he charmed me, I was sure I could do the same for him. Last night, we connected. I could make him understand.

I felt less sure of that when he opened the door to our room and stared over my head until I walked past him.

The door closed heavy and firm, sealing us inside. Turning, I took in the harsh set of his jaw and the dark hint in his eyes.

"Why did you do it, Serena?" He glowered down at me, his arms crossed over his chest.

I kicked off my shoes. "What do you mean?"

"Why did you fuck me?"

I blinked. It wasn't the beginning of the conversation that I was expecting.

"You—you know why." I stammered my voice thin.

He must have seen my uneasiness in my body language because he asked, "Are you scared?"

"I don't know what to make of you like this."

Sighing a deep breath, he took a few deliberate steps around me and the bed, placing himself on the other side of the room and giving me access to the exit. "I'm livid, Serena, but I won't hurt you."

Nodding down at my feet, I mumbled, "Okay. Just tell me what's going on."

"I saw your text messages." Normally his sentences were threaded with playfulness and warmth, but now he spoke with measured control. "I wasn't lookin' through your phone if that's what you're thinking. It popped up as I was closing the map app."

"I didn't accuse you of that." I squared my shoulders and met his eye. "So, now you know someone's stealing, and we know it's not you. I'm sure it was shocking to see that, but you were never actually a suspect."

"Oh, don't I feel grateful. Thank you for clearing that up." The measured control from before was taken over by venom. "Why did my name even come up if you didn't think it was me? Why were you *spying* on me, if you didn't think it was me?"

"That was poor timing. I wasn't spying on you. Will was being mostly sarcastic."

A muscle flexed in his jaw. "*Mostly* sarcastic?"

"Yes, Daire, mostly." Impatience was beginning to weave into my tone and my words piled on top of each other as they flew out of my mouth without much consideration. "I wasn't *spying*, but I had my eyes open. I wasn't trying to *get* information, but if I found information, I would keep it. It was unlikely it was you."

"Why did you fuck me?" he repeated.

"You know why. I don't understand why you're asking me this."

He tilted his head, and his stare was sharp enough to cut. "Did you fuck me for information?"

"What?" I said, shocked.

"Did you fuck me for information?"

"I heard you the first time."

"With how you've been making me repeat myself, I just assumed."

"No, I did not *fuck* you for information. Jesus, what do you think I am?"

"So, you never suspected me?"

"I didn't say that." As soon as the words left my mouth, I wanted to take them back. My thoughts were more nuanced than that. In truth, I wasn't thinking clearly through my anger. Not when he thought I'd slept with him to manipulate him. Not when I'd felt something beautiful between us and he was painting it into something detestable.

His chest compressed as he breathed out through his nose—as if my words had struck him in the heart.

"I didn't think it was you," I said, my voice calmer. "I just didn't have proof that it wasn't. This was new information to me a couple of days ago, and I wasn't sure what to think."

"But you fucked me anyway... even though you thought I could be stealing from my work." His words were quieter—raw.

"I didn't think it was you," I repeated.

"You say that like that absolves you."

"I don't need absolution."

The wrinkles in his forehead deepened as he lifted his eyebrows. "You don't? Then why do I feel so used?"

I lifted my chin. "I don't know, why do you?"

He tilted his head, considering me. "I don't believe that you'd think there was a chance that I did this, and not try to get *something* from me."

My mouth hung open as I searched for the next words to say. I shrugged. "Yeah, but... but you could have said something to prove you were innocent."

"I opened up to you last night, you know. I... I don't do that easily."

Guilt sank like lead in my stomach. "Everything that you thought last night was... is what it was. I wasn't using you. I wasn't trying to get anything from you."

He nodded. The movement warped into his head shaking. "I'm going to sleep in the car."

"You don't have to do that—"

"No." He let out a humorless laugh. "That's how I know this doesn't mean the same thing to you as it does to me. I can't share a bed with you if I can't trust you." He swallowed and looked down at his empty hands. "But then that's not really fair, not when..." He straightened and met my eyes. "Serena, I quit."

"Okay..." I resisted rubbing my clammy palms on my pants. "I just... I don't think you should do that right now. Take a couple of nights to calm down. I think you'll see things more clearly. You're valued at Garcia. Don't do anything rash."

A sneer marred his beautiful face, turning it cynical, and for a nerve-wracking moment, I thought he might tell me that he was involved with the embezzling. "Rash? Like fucking my boss?"

Heat rose up my neck.

"Honestly, I was leaving anyway. I just wasn't going to tell you like this."

For a moment my mouth just hung open. "Is that why you botched the presentation?"

"Botched the presentation? You should be falling over yourself to give me a reference and push me out the door. This does not look good for you or Garcia—you fucked me, made me trust you, *spied* on me, and now you're accusing me of not doing my job? How do you think that looks, Serena?"

I closed my mouth so quickly that my teeth clicked.

"Are you going public—"

"No." He folded his arms over his chest as if to protect himself. "Because whatever it was to you, it meant something to me."

I figured neither of us wanted me to tell him that it mattered too me to, so I didn't. "Where will you go?"

"I've been in communication with Sustainably Green. I think they'll take me on."

"You should have disclosed that," I accused. "That's a conflict of interest. You should have *never* been on this trip. You should have mentioned this before we left."

"It's not. Hutchington can be treated like any other potential client I've spoken to—"

"But you know my image plan."

"If knowledge on Hutchington is a conflict of interest, then so are about half of my Garcia clients."

"You'll cost us Hutchington."

"Aren't you sick and tired of helping people *look* like they give a shit? I am. I'm sick of myself over it. I can't do it anymore. I've signed non-disclosures with Garcia, and I'll honor them. But I'm done. And I want you to give me a reference."

I actually barked a laugh. "You've got some goddamn gall. You're more likely to get sued by Garcia than get a reference from me."

His face contorted in pain, and his eyes filled with betrayal. "Jesus Christ." Staring over my shoulder at nothing, he said, "You should give me the reference because I've done a good job for you. The rest of it, I don't know."

"You should go out to the car." I had to fight against the tears in my eyes, and the shudder in my breath as he gathered up his clothes. He shoved them haphazardly into his suitcase and carried it to the door.

With my back to him, I said, "I won't give you that reference."

It didn't even sound like he slowed his stride as he left the room and me behind.

Chapter Thirteen

Serena

I was sure the hotel bed felt too big only because I'd slept in it with Daire, but then I'd been sleeping in my bed at home for the past six nights, and it felt too big without him even though he'd never slept there. In my sleep I traveled the length of my mattress, searching for the warmth of his skin, somehow cold even though most nights I woke up sweating. My dreams were full of nightmares—the most haunting was of Daire and me alone on a plane holding hands just before I shoved him out into freefall.

The nightmares were almost better than the dreams that made me wake up panting and needing.

I read and reread the email he'd sent me and Louisa giving his resignation, not that it was specific.

Please consider this my resignation, effective immediately.

Sincerely,

Daire O'Dowd

He must have had it typed out on the plane, just waiting to hit send when we landed back in Chicago.

It wasn't like he was leaving *me*. There was no *me* to leave. But that was exactly how it felt.

Louisa had called me before I'd reached the row of taxis waiting to travel from the airport to the city. I'd answered my phone and pretended not to see him climbing into the backseat of a different yellow car. Even though, I'd wanted to watch him. Knowing it was likely the last time I'd see him, and even with everything that made me bleed.

"Hi, Louisa," I'd answered.

"What's going on? Why is Daire leaving?" She'd sounded slightly winded, and there had been the quiet whir of her stationary bike in the background.

I'd told her about Sustainably Green, but omitted most everything else. It really didn't feel like her business that he and I had slept together. I did tell her about him knowing about the embezzlement, but despite all of the ugliness between us, I couldn't see him telling anyone. Withholding information from Louisa could make mitigating the public perception more challenging, if I was my client I'd be furious. But I wasn't my client. And I didn't want to tell her.

She'd listened before saying, "Well, fuck."

"Yeah."

"I'll talk to Mr. Hutchington, and explain that Daire is no longer a member of the team... fuck, and that he's moving to Sustainably Green. I wish you'd told me this last night."

Sitting on the vinyl seats in the back of the taxi, I'd stared out the window missing my apartment. "I know."

"It's not like you. Is there something else?"

I'd pinched my lips together and shook my head, even though she couldn't see. "No. It was just an exhausting couple of days..."

It was a weak excuse.

"We might have been able to get in front of this if you'd called me last night."

It was good she hadn't been able to see how I'd rolled my eyes. She would have fired him, and we could have controlled the narrative around his termination. I'd known that. I'd even considered making the phone call more than once, but I couldn't. I didn't want to ruin Daire's plans or his future.

"I know," I'd said.

She'd sighed. "Well, here we are."

I'd modeled my career and much of my life around Louisa's example—a woman fully devoted to her profession and building her company. I didn't regret that decision; I'd been happy to do it. But as I'd ridden in the taxi and the Chicago skyline grew nearer, I hadn't felt happy. I felt... I wasn't sure.

Six days. I hadn't seen him or heard from him in six days. And I still felt not happy.

I was a grown woman. I'd had flings before, some that ended well, and some that ended crying and screaming. I'd lick my wounds and keep moving until they didn't hurt anymore. But every day I got further from burying our not-a-relationship, the more I felt it knocking and scratching from inside the coffin. There were stupid little things that I couldn't let go of, like what would he think of my apartment, with my dirty dishes left on the coffee table and my clothes scattered on the floor? How would we have spent our nights? Would we have snuggled on my sofa and watched TV? Or would he have opened a sci-fi paperback while I read one of my romances?

What would our relationship have looked like?

I only had a short amount of time where he'd been more than the man I coveted, when I had permission to touch him and taste him. But the loss of that fleeting time... I missed him. And the missing wasn't easing with time. Instead, it scraped away my protective shell leaving me feeling exposed and heart sore.

"Rena," Willow called from her desk. She sounded like it wasn't the first time she'd said my name.

"Hm?" I blinked.

She bit her lower lip and pointed to a pencil on the floor near her office chair, her casted leg up on a little stool. "Can you pick that up for me?"

Even in my sour mood, I had to laugh. "Sure."

I walked around my desk and across the office. Guiltily, Will handed me a tissue. I lifted a questioning eyebrow.

"I was using it to itch my leg."

"Oh... that's..."

"Gross, yeah. I can't wait for this stupid cast to come off."

Grabbing the pencil with the tissue, I sat it on her desk wondering how many writing utensils were trapped inside of the hard plaster. Recalling Daire telling her about when he had a cast as a boy. A *lad* with a broken arm, and a hard man for a dad, and how he wanted to do worthwhile work.

The feeling I'd been trying to place for days became clear. Disappointment. But not in him. He had been a good employee, excellent even. He'd put the firm in a tough spot with Hutchington, but withholding his plans was—at best a gray area ethically. Giving him a reference was still unadvised, but it felt like the right choice.

But instead of seeing him leaving the firm as separate from leaving me, I was connecting it all into one. And it made me disgusted with myself.

"What just clicked?" Will's question broke through my daze.

"Clicked?"

"You have that look when you've figured something out."

I nodded. Striding to the door, I closed it. "Can you help me figure out who's in charge of hiring and interviews at Sustainably Green here in town?"

She opened her contact list up. I doubted that she had the email to the actual person we were looking for, but she'd know people who did. I sat back in my seat, opened my email, and began drafting. It took a few more minutes for me to complete the body of the email than it did for Willow to find the contact that we needed.

I called their office administrator as she read through the body of my email.

"Hello, Molly Jessop's office," a young woman answered.

"Hello, this is Serena Jackson. I'm with Garcia Public Relations. I was curious if Daire O'Dowd was still in the interview process."

"Uh, I'm sorry, I don't think that I can share that information."

"Of course, excuse me. I'm sending an email over. If Ms. Jessop is still considering Mr. O'Dowd, I'd greatly appreciate that she be given this email."

"Uh... okay. I can make sure that she receives it."

"Thank you so much for your time." I hung up.

Willow nodded at the text on my screen. "It's good. Louisa will be pissed... but it's good."

My stomach was tied in knots, but I hovered the cursor over the send button, and through the power of the Internet, it left my outbox to land in Molly Jessop's inbox.

"I'll talk to Louisa." I sounded more confident than I felt.

"Is he worth it?" Will asked.

"It was just the right thing to do."

She shook her head, her face grim.

"Do you think she'll fire me?"

After a moment, Willow shook her head again. "No, but it won't be good."

Louisa's office door was open, as it usually was at the end of the day. I tapped a knuckle on the door jam, and she looked up over the tops of her glasses, the screen of the tablet in her hands reflected off of their lenses.

"Rena?" Louisa sat on her black leather sofa with her patent black heels on the rug and her legs crossed at the ankles on the cushions. Unlike the rest of the office suite, her space was monochromatic. Stark clear lines. Black and white. Just like the workings of her mind.

I mustered a half smile. "Hey, do you have a minute?"

"Of course, have a seat." She set the tablet on the coffee table and shifted her feet to the floor. When I sat on the opposite end of the sofa, she fixed her dark brown eyes on me, soft wrinkles crinkling their corners with her comforting smile. "Is everything okay?"

I stared at the stark lines on the white rug as I considered how to answer. Every time I imagined this conversation in the past couple of hours, I couldn't see a clear path. Louisa was predictable in that she would always put the firm first. And until recently, she would have likely described me the same way. I hadn't made any catastrophic decisions before, but what I'd just done had the potential to be dangerous. There had been a clear shift in my actions, and I didn't know what she would make of it.

Sighing, I said, "I wrote Daire a reference for Sustainably Green."

She went eerily still. "Did Hutchington tell you that they spoke?"

"Daire and Mr. Hutchington?"

She narrowed her eyes. "You didn't know?"

"No. What did they talk about?"

"I'm not sure. Hutchington backed off on some of the more obnoxious elements of the negotiation. He did say that he liked Daire's 'free-agent mindset.'" She shook her head and considered me. "It was still a terrible decision. We are keeping Hutchington by the skin of our teeth, we could lose him outright. We need to be perfect."

"I know. But Daire helped us?"

"For now, and it only got us so much goodwill. Shit, Rena, if Lawrence & Lawrence find out about this..." I could practically see her internal crisis management. I'd known her long enough to know that the thought of losing Hutchington was less than the horror of her longtime rival Sean Lawrence getting leverage over her. They constantly found unfindable information on each other, and my helping a publicist gain a position at a company that could hurt our newest and largest account would not be good for Garcia Public Relations.

She breathed in deeply and held her breath for a beat. "I am already doing everything I can to keep... *everything* quiet, and you do this without even consulting me."

"I knew you wouldn't approve, but it was the right thing for me to do."

"Christ." She shook her head. "I know you liked him, but we all did."

I didn't point out that my feelings for Daire were likely different than hers. "He was an exceptional employee, and he didn't deserve to leave without our endorsement."

She lifted one perfectly arched black eyebrow. "This has nothing to do with the date you had to cancel when he first started?"

"No... It does not. I did this because it was the right thing to do. But... if given the opportunity, I would pursue a relationship with him."

She stared out the window, slowly shaking her head. "Fuck, Rena."

I was privy to an openness that she wouldn't have shown if even one other person had been in the room.

"I know." I hated disappointing her, and I wanted to apologize. But I wouldn't. Not when I knew I was right. Not when I was being honest.

"I don't know what to say."

I leaned toward her over my crossed knees holding her gaze. "I have never regretted my choices in regards to the firm. You've made it easy to put its interests first, but I would have regretted it this time." I looked back to the stark lines of the rug. "Our morals will most likely continue to align, but I saw—" I cut off at the memory of the betrayal on Daire's face. "I had to make it right."

"I'm going to need time to think about this. I don't... I don't know what to say to you right now."

Standing, I wiped my sweaty palms on my slacks. "I'm available to talk when you're ready."

I was almost to the door when she asked, "What does it feel like doing this for you, and not the firm?"

It was an honest question, without any malice. I considered Louisa, slouched against the arm of the sofa. It was as if I was seeing for the first time the dark circles under her eyes. A chink in her impeccable armor. She was just over ten years older than me, but I'd never seen those years appear so heavy as I did at that moment.

I shrugged. "Honestly, it feels right. If it didn't, I would be miserable right now."

She swallowed, and the tendons in her neck stuck out more than they had a few weeks ago.

"Are you alright?" I asked.

Sitting up straight, her armor fit back into place. "It's just been a rough month. The *discovery*" —"embezzlement" hung unsaid between us—"and..." She shook her head. "I'll take an easy weekend and get some rest. I'm not happy with you, Serena, but I think I understand more than I thought I would."

"If you need someone to talk to..."

"That's kind of you, but I'm okay. We'll discuss all of this later."

"Good night, Louisa."

"Good night."

Chapter Fourteen

♥

Daire

I wandered block after block, chasing my thoughts after my second interview. Molly Jessop had been coldly professional in our first interview, but during the second she'd been warmer—not necessarily friendly, but rumor was that was her way. The shift in temperature was made clearer when she said, "Serena Jackson likes you."

My heart lodged somewhere at the base of my throat, somewhere it was not supposed to be judging by how hard it was to swallow. "I'm sorry?"

Her long, slender braids fell gracefully from her shoulder as she nodded. "I got her reference letter about an hour ago." She raised her thin eyebrows. "She thinks really highly of you."

"She was a pleasure to work with. I learned a lot from her, honestly. I don't know if I've ever seen anyone more committed to what they do," I'd said without any falsehood. Working with Serena hadn't been the problem; it was when intimacy and trustworthiness came into our dynamic that the trouble began. I wondered what the letter could have stated that would make Mrs. Jessop mention it at all.

I waited at a crosswalk for the light to change as the Red Line train rattled overhead, deafening all other sounds than the ones in my head. I wondered what was in the letter, but even more so, I wondered why Serena wrote it at all. She'd said she wouldn't. She'd been outraged that I would ask. She'd said I was more likely to get sued than I was to get a reference.

For the past few days, I'd turned our fight over and over in my mind—while I tried to study the social climate of Sustainably Green, while I worked out, while I tried to read. While I laid awake in bed, feeling the stab of betrayal anew.

But then she'd written that letter.

Taking my phone out of my pocket, I unlocked the screen before locking it again and putting it back in my pocket. I repeated the process one more time before the light turned and I joined the few other pedestrians crossing the street.

It was midday on a Friday, and traffic was growing denser with weekend travelers, but I kept heading north in the opposite direction of my apartment. I needed to clear my head and put my thoughts in an order that I could understand—they jumped from bitterness to hope with such velocity I had emotional whiplash.

I knew what I wanted Serena's letter to mean, and the fact that I wanted to trust her frightened me. People rarely asked more than face value from me. I was the reflection they wanted to see, and I liked it that way. I liked being around people but protected from them. But I let Serena peel back the facade and I knew she liked what she saw there. Under her gaze, I hadn't felt at risk of harm.

But you were harmed, an angry voice whispered from the back of my mind. The voice that sounded most like my father. It was always there to remind me to pull back. To remain hidden. I'd ignored it... for her. I didn't know if I could do it again, not after six days of heartache and feeling the walls crumble atop me when doubting her came in. Except that wasn't fair either, she'd admitted to being watchful of me, but the same would likely be true of anyone else in the office. They didn't know who was embezzling and they were probably suspicious of everyone.

I halted in the middle of the sidewalk and the man behind me had to come to a stop to not run into me.

"I'm sorry," I mumbled and moved to stand next to the nearest skyscraper.

He grumbled something that sounded like, "Fucking idiot," but kept walking.

The pad of my thumb left a clammy halo on the screen of my phone as I opened Serena's contact and tapped out a text.

Her reply followed seconds later.

I kept walking in the direction I'd been going, following a magnetic pull that would lead me straight to her.

The bar next to her office had canopies over the outdoor seating. I'd likely avoid sunburn. At least if our conversation went poorly, it'd only be my heart that was burned to a crisp. I looked up the street, at the cars glinting like the sun off of the lake.

She stepped out of the front door of her building, her tan skin gold against her dark hair. The sight of her made my brain fizzle and my fingers long to touch her. She lifted her hand in a wave that was at once unsure and not awkward, a balance that only she could be pulled off. I waved back much more awkwardly.

She went to the front door of the bar, and a few moments later she was outside on the patio just a few feet away from me. We just stared at each other at first, before I stood—scraping the chair against the concrete with a screech.

I'd thought the last time I would see her was out of the corner of my eye as she lowered into the taxi at the airport. We might cross paths for work, but it was less likely now that I was in the nonprofit arena. And yes, we both lived in Chicago, but Chicago was a big city, and we were just two people.

There were five feet between us; I could see the strands of hair that had slipped from her bun. She took a step closer.

Three. The shape of her lips drew in fine detail. Another step. One. Her eyes green and hesitant.

I pulled out her chair with one hand, scraping it too loudly across the concrete.

She smirked, and my heart was caught on the curve of her lips like a hook. "Doing the chair thing?"

"Force of habit." My voice sounded rougher than I expected.

Her lips fell back to neutral. "Thank you."

The urge to tell her that it was a habit I wanted to only do for her was so strong. But I needed information or reassurance; I wasn't sure which exactly. I held the urge back.

We sat. The waitress came by, saving us from what I was sure would have been an uncomfortable silence. Serena ordered a rosé, and I got a pint of lager.

When we were alone again, I didn't wait for the silence to fall between us. "Why did you write the recommendation?"

Her chest rose with a breath. "You asked for it, and you deserved it." She chewed on her bottom lip then went on. "I was angry. I don't *love* how you left, but you're outstanding at your job. I hope you have the career you want." She leveled me with a stare that made it clear she was watching my every movement. "Why did you talk to Hutchington?"

It had taken several phone calls to actually get on the phone with him. I figured if I dropped my name, someone was bound to know that the old man had a bone to pick with me. When we'd finally got talking, I'd walked a fine line between groveling and charm before I knew I had convinced him that Garcia Public Relations were not responsible for the moves I'd made. Then I'd given him dirt on me, some information about the strife between me and Da—it both explained why I made the choice I did, but would also hurt my image if it became public.

"Ammunition," I explained, "if I ever break the NDA we have."

It was a risky move, but it was also the only way I knew how to make things right for Garcia—for Serena.

I sighed. "I don't *love* the way I left either. I really... I put you in a bad spot."

"Thank you."

I rested my chin on my fist and considered her. Her spine was straight, and her shoulders were back. She met my gaze without wavering. Anyone else would think that she was completely confident, but I'd seen this posture before. I would have bet anything that there was more.

"The letter was purely business?" I asked.

She sighed. "Has it ever been purely business between us?"

"True. Then what else is it?"

"An apology, I guess."

There were a couple of things she could have been apologizing for—lord knew I had plenty of amends to make—so I waited for her to go on.

The waitress came back with our drinks, and we thanked her.

After taking a sip of her wine, Serena said, "I didn't sleep with you to exploit you, but I had been paying attention, seeing if there was anything that would confirm your involvement or innocence. I would have felt like my trust was violated too." I watched the condensation on her glass wind down its edge as she spoke, but met her eyes when she grew quiet. "I'm sorry, Daire."

"Thank you." I wrapped both of my hands around my drink. "I'm sorry too. I should have left Garcia on proper terms."

"I understand why you didn't."

"Honestly, I've been very embarrassed by my behavior there."

She shrugged. "Thanks."

Her neck worked as she swallowed another sip.

"Are you any closer to going to the authorities? About..." I talked around the subject but she obviously understood.

Looking through her eyelashes, she considered me. "Am I safe to talk about this?"

I nodded. "You're safe with me, Serena."

Her shoulders lowered a fraction. "We still don't have a firm timeline, and all of the accounts are pretty random."

My eyebrows pinched together. "That sounds like it'd have to be someone in accounting then."

"Yeah."

"Miya wouldn't..."

"No, she was the one who pointed all of this out. It would make her a terrible criminal."

"Of course, forget I even—"

"No, it's okay. I'm sure there's been a conversation that my name has been thrown into too. We're all just watching each other, but we're not actually getting anywhere. If we don't figure out something soon, we're going to have to go to the police."

I cringed and hoped that it wouldn't come to that. That could end a small firm like Garcia Public Relations.

A car horn blared right next to us as if to put an end to that conversation.

"I got the job. Just waiting on the paperwork." I looked up at her through my brow.

Her face lit up with a wide smile. "Yeah?"

"Yeah, your recommendation was a large part of that. What did you say in it?"

"Uh... you know... the normal platitudes."

I scoffed. "Sure, that's why Jessop mentioned it to me and why it packed such a punch. Because of *normal platitudes*."

"I mean, yeah, I told them how you're fantastic in every situation, how you elevate your work environment, how you're capable of adapting. How... you'd be missed."

"I don't know if I deserve all of—"

"You do."

"Thank you."

Tentatively, I reached across the table. My heart pounded in my chest as I curled my hand around hers, and ran my thumb on the back of her knuckles.

"Serena, I don't want this to be the last time I see you," I spoke to our joined hands. I wanted to be strong enough to meet her eyes, but if she turned me down, I couldn't bear for her to see the look on my face.

"I want to see you again too." Her mouth was spread wide, and her eyes were so bright they rivaled the summer sun.

"Can I take you out on that date?"

"Yes."

With my free hand, I cupped the back of her neck. She leaned toward me, and our mouths met. She tasted of sweet wine and promise. This woman who made every hair on my body stand on end, and the blood rush inside of my veins, was willing to risk her public image for me. I understood what I could cost her, and I didn't take it lightly.

I wouldn't make her regret this choice. I would make this risk worthwhile. The past few days had given me perspective on what it was to miss her. I didn't want to miss her ever again.

I was ensnared by her and entirely charmed to be there.

Epilogue

♥

Serena

By the time that I showed up at the bar next to our office building, Daire and Willow already had a table on the patio. A couple of weeks ago, Willow's plaster cast had been removed and was replaced by a soft cast. She'd started her physical therapy shortly after. Which was good; she had been getting antsy and the exercise was obviously helping her mind.

"Daire, he is so hot," she was saying. She held her hands on either side of her eyes like blinders, but I knew behind her hands her eyes were huge and her face was glowing red. "Like... I try not to notice. I try—I *try* not to notice. But I *notice*."

He looked in my direction as soon as I entered the patio, a smirk on his face. We kissed—a polite hello, even though as soon as our mouths met it was torture to pull away. It would be one thing if we made out a bit after everyone had a couple of drinks and the rest of our group was there, but it'd be pretty rude with just Will. So, I sat in the empty chair next to him.

"Yes, I have no idea what it's like to be attracted to someone you aren't supposed to be," he said dryly looking at me.

"And the positions," she continued, her eyes like saucers. "The positions we have to do, and his hands are kinda every-where—like in a totally professional way, but they're very good hands. Oh my god, he's my doctor. I have *very* inappropriate feelings."

"You should just find a different office." I'd given her that advice before. It was part of the cycle: she attended PT, then freaked out about her hot doctor, then calmed down, said she was being ridiculous just in time to attend PT again and start the cycle anew.

"I know I should, but it's not his fault he's hot."

"I'm sure it's quite the hardship," Daire deadpanned.

"Well, how do you handle being irresistibly hot?" I asked.

"I manage."

Our Friday evening cocktails had become a thing after we celebrated his first week at Sustainably Green. Lexi, Miya and Willow had joined us. It'd been a little weird at first, but everyone had settled into having him around after a couple of drinks. They'd folded him into our group as if he was our missing fifth friend.

"Hi," Lexi called to us from the patio entrance, holding the door open for Miya.

She took the seat next to me and, after a single glance at Willow asked, "So, we're talking about the hot doctor?"

Willow's shoulders sagged, and her head fell back. "He's so hot."

Stiffly, Lexi patted Willow's shoulder. "There, there."

Miya, Daire and I laughed, but Will glared at Lex.

Daire and I stayed until our hands roamed a bit too much and our friends threw wadded-up cocktail napkins at us. Then we made quick goodbyes and hailed a taxi. In the backseat we were as subtle as two horny drunk people trying to be subtle could be, but his hand was up my skirt far enough that his fingertips brushed my panties. My fingers fondled his hard shaft from the inside of his pocket.

So real subtle.

He ran his palm up and down the curve of my ass as I fumbled to unlock my door, my brain foggy with alcohol and arousal. I pressed back against his hips, and he ground into me.

His hand slipped around my front to draw a circle around my puckered nipple. "Open the door, Tulip, or your neighbors are gonna get an eyeful."

"I'm trying, but you're distracting."

He repeated his circle, and my knees buckled, my cunt slick with need.

"Distracting," I whispered.

But he didn't stop. Eventually, by miracle alone, I managed to unlock the door. We stumbled over the shoes I'd left on the floor earlier. He guided me to my sofa.

"Get your skirt outta my way," he growled in my ear.

I whimpered and hiked my skirt over my hips obediently.

He made a sound of appreciation at the back of his throat that I felt down my spine. Filling his hands with my ass, he rubbed his cock still inside of his pants down my slit.

Arching my back, I moaned.

The sound of his leather belt sliding open increased the yearning winding in my core. A few moments later, his naked legs met mine. He eased me to kneel on the sofa with my hands braced on the wall behind it. When he filled me, I saw stars.

He groaned. "So fucking wet. Did you get this wet at the bar when I kissed your ear? Or in the taxi, with my hand up your skirt while I tried my damnedest not to finger you?"

His hips rolled, pulling him out and pushing him in, and each time he hit a place inside of me that made me cry out.

"I asked a question, Tulip. When was it?"

"Yes," I whined.

"That doesn't answer—"

"All of the time," I breathed, my hips bucking as he pushed me nearer to the edge. "All of the time. I'm wet for you all of the time. Fuck. Please, more."

His fingers sank into my hips, and he speared into me over and over, my cheek pressed against my wall. I fell apart, and he came right after me. I collapsed onto the cushions when he stepped away. He returned with a towel and wiped his come off of my upper thighs.

He pressed a kiss to my temple. "Come on, my love, let's go to bed."

I let him lead me to my room, a goofy smile on my face.

"What are you grinning at?" he asked, laying on the mattress next to me.

"You called me 'my love.'" My voice sounded far away and dreamy even to me.

He pulled me tight against his chest. "A title well deserved. I love you."

"I love you too."

Never Has She Ever sneak peak

Willow

"That's nice. Firm."

Laying on my stomach, I exhaled a shuddering breath. My heated face was hidden as his hand on my calf moved lower. His strong fingers encircled my ankle, and a shiver rolled over my scalp and then continued down my spine. His other hand shifted from my knee to my inner thigh. My heart pounded in my ears—a throbbing between my legs made me want to whimper.

"Flex," he directed. "Push—*easy*."

I instantly followed his command and lightened my resistance against him.

"That's right."

His voice was baritone silk—every affirmation slipped over me, smooth and slick. "Breathe."

My lungs filled with a quick gust of air as I realized I'd been holding my breath. With it came his clean scent, laundry detergent and soap. A whimper escaped my lips. My eyes widened at the black mat a few feet below me.

His fingers twitched on my thigh and his grip on my ankle tightened. "That feel good? Is it too deep?"

"Good," I answered, my voice slightly higher then normal. "I'm good. It feels good. Keep going."

I was, totally good... except my face was on fire from embarrassment, the seam of my yoga pants kept rubbing on my swollen clit, and I should *not* lust after my physical therapist—but I was absolutely lusting after my physical therapist.

Except all of that, everything was fine.

"Only a few more minutes." He reassured me.

During my session last week, I'd stopped referring to him as Dr. Vasile in my thoughts. I'd hoped it would depersonalize him. *He* could be anyone. I could picture my old bus driver the constantly scowling bulldog-faced Mr. Hopper instead of Dr. Vasile and his devastating rich brown eyes and high cheekbones with the black scruff of his five o-clock shadow. The depersonalization didn't seem to be working.

I focused on following his instructions through the cool-down stretches. Turning my brain on auto-pilot, and tried to find the off switch for my desire.

I'd picked his practice because it was in my insurance's network and located in the same building as my work. The choice had been a blessing and a curse ever since. He was a great doctor, but he was also devastatingly hot.

The mobility in my healed leg was significantly better than it had been when my cast had come off weeks ago. It also wasn't like it had been before the car accident that had broken it.

It had been an unsettling couple of months. First, the car crash that broke my leg and uprooted my normally very active lifestyle, and then the discovery of money being embezzled from the PR firm I worked at.

Just the thought of it had my shoulders tensing, and my fist clenching—the edges of my nails dug into my palms.

Right before I left for this appointment, Miya our account-ing manager found yet another fake consulting account. It only made me madder that I'd have to wait until Monday to get a look at it. I inhaled slowly through my nose and out my mouth, to keep my breathing from accelerating.

"Hey," Dr. Vasile said letting go of my leg and taking a few steps back. "I think we're done."

I allowed myself one more breath before pushing to sit on the massage table, swinging my legs over the edge. "So, how'd I do, Doc?"

"You tell me, are you okay?"

I met his deep brown eyes surrounded by the longest thick-est lashes I'd ever seen and shrugged. "Yeah."

He raised a black eyebrow and glanced at my fists pressed into the vinyl seat on either side of my hips.

Clearing my throat, I shook my head and smiled in what I hoped looked self-deprecating. I ran my palms on my outer thighs. "It's okay, I just... probably walked more than I should have yesterday."

"It can be hard at this stage to know when you've over-ex-erted yourself. Your progress is great, but watch it."

"I will."

He considered me for a moment. "Are you sure there's nothing else?"

"What else would there be?" Years of training in public relations helped me mask anxiety that lay just below the surface. It was a handy trick—controlling my outer persona, but it came with its tethers. Sometimes I concealed feelings that I shouldn't, but in this case, I couldn't think of anything medically relevant that he could be talking about. Instead, I had a flashing fear that he'd picked up on just how much my body responded to his nearness.

He sat on the rolling stool with his legs spread and placed his elbows on his thighs. "A lot of people suffer from PTSD after collisions. Have you had any trouble sleeping or night-mares? Flashbacks?"

Relief rushed through my system, and I shook my head. "No, I'm good, thank you for asking."

"Okay, then you're done. This was the last session as expected." He stood and reached a hand out to me. "It was great to help you, Willow."

I put my feet on the black mat and took his hand. "If I am having nightmares, do I get to have more physical therapy?"

His full lips quirked up to one side. "No, but you could get psychological therapy and they could help with coping mechanisms."

I swallowed slipping my hand from his. "Drats."

He smiled politely.

I folded my arms across my chest. "Pretend like I said, 'Damnit.' Or whatever it is that people our age say and not everyone's favorite grandma."

"My grandma would have said, 'Fuck.'"

I snorted.

"That's a joke I can say now that you aren't my patient, right?" He tilted his head and there was the smallest glint of something new in his eyes—something promising.

In the time it took me to blink in surprise and try to gather my nerves to ask my hot doctor out on a date, his expression sobered into its normal polite bedside manner. "Anyway, I'm glad I was able to help you."

"Uh, totally. Thank you."

"You don't even have to checkout, you can grab your things and..." he shrugged his broad shoulders, "never come back."

"Right. Thank you again." I turned a little faster than necessary and almost tripped on the leg of the massage table. Exiting the training room, I didn't look over my shoulder to see if he'd noticed my clumsiness. I waved to the desk worker, a middle-aged woman who had never warmed to me. She didn't wave back. My keys were in the cubby I'd dropped them in before my appointment. My car's key was still on the chain even though my car hadn't moved from its parking spot since the guy at the body shop parked it there. I usually drove home to northwestern Michigan often enough to justify owning a car in Chicago.

But those trips were getting less and less frequent. I could probably look into car rentals instead. I'd figure it out after my sister's birthday party in a couple of weeks.

I shoved my keys into the pocket of my leggings.

Glancing over my shoulder, I saw Dr. Vasile put a chart under his arm and pull his phone from his scrubs. I could just leave, maybe I should, but then I might never see him again. Even working in the same building, we'd never bumped into each other—I would have remembered him.

Since I'd probably wouldn't see him again, what was the harm in trying one at least once?

"Miss," the woman at the front desk called as I pushed open the door to the training room. I walked past her as she continued to yell.

He looked up from the phone in his hand. "Hey, did you forget something?"

The doors opened behind me again, and he held up a hand. "It's okay, Alice, I've got this."

Alice didn't look like it was okay, she looked like she would throw me over her shoulder a chuck me out onto the sidewalk. Her thin lips pinched tight, and she glared at me before going back to her post.

His dark eyebrows lifted, and his dark eyes met mine. "She's very efficient, and I don't know how this place would run without her... but she..." He paused considering his words. "Customer service isn't her best skill."

The dry response of, *couldn't tell*, seemed rude so instead, I said, "It's good she's efficient."

"What can I help you wi—" he cut himself off at the buzz from the phone in his pocket.

"Do you need to get that?"

He half cringed, half rolled his eyes. "No, it's just my roommate."

"Argument over who ate who's leftovers?"

He snorted. "No, she just let me know that she has someone over."

"Is that a big deal?"

"Well... she's my ex and I'm trying to find a different place, but... Anyway, I don't want to go home if she has a guy there, you know?"

I was more than capable of seeing an opportunity when it was right in front of me. "Wanna get drinks with me and my friends?"

"Really? I don't want to intrude."

"Don't worry about it, I was coming in here to invite you anyway."

He smirked and that wonderful *something* came back into his eyes. "You were?"

My stomach was full of butterflies, their wings flitting anxiously. "Yup."

"If I won't be an intrusion."

"You won't. My friends have only heard really good things about you."

"You've told your friends about me?"

It felt like my tongue swelled inside of my mouth, but somehow I found a way to speak. "Of course, they were concerned about my... health."

I left unsaid all of the times I lamented my giant crush/lust for my incredibly hot/sweet doctor.

His lips pursed like he was fighting a smile, and mine did the same. Nodding, he said, "Then I guess I should report your clean bill of health in person."

Acknowledgements

Put on your seatbelts, friends, there's a list of people who deserve so many thank yous!

Sarah at Lopt & Cropt Editing, thank you so much for helping this story through its growing pains. Rae Shawn, you went through and fixed all of my grammar issues, and gave this book a professional polish. Kate Prior, I love my cover! You did such a beautiful job.

To my amazing husband, you are so supportive and you don't give yourself the credit you deserve there. You have prioritized my writing not only monetarily, but also with the time and mental energy it takes from me—there have been many a distracted conversation during which you would like input but my mind is working through a scene. Just like everything in my life, I'm so happy to be doing this with you. Danielle, my amazing friend, who finds time to read my stories and always loves them. You are so many things to me, but you're also the voice I listen to when the imposter syndrome kicks in. To my lovely Smut Coven, you have helped my writing grow so much in the past two years. 2020 would have been so much darker without you all being amazing and ridiculous. I'm so grateful for you, and I don't know what I would do without you. To my aunts who supported my love of reading, even when it ventured into romance at a young age. Thank you for always encouraging me to write. Thank you for bringing me to book signings and sharing your vast library. To my friends with our group text, and being excited when I share my "Your excited writer friend" moments.

I guess I should probably thank my mom too, huh? If you know me, you know that my mom is awesome. She's silly and creative, and so much fun. But she is also passionate and believes without any astrics attached that your dreams are valid. That *my* dreams are valid, achievable and worthy. The list of reasons that my mom deserves a thank you is so long, but I'm just going to say thank you for instilling in me an unwavering belief in myself. Your best was enough. Thanks, Mom.

Marty Vee in the Wild

♥

Marty Vee lives in Michigan with her husband, two kids, a dog, and two cats. She loves reading, and hiking, and generally being outside.

Vee is for Romance Readers Group

https://www.facebook.com/groups/1161878791021065
The Tiktok

https://www.tiktok.com/@martyveeauthur
Instagram

https://www.instagram.com/martyveeauthor/
Twitter

https://twitter.com/MartyVeeAuthor
Romance Writer's Therapy Podcast

https://romancewriterstherapy.buzzsprout.com/